Treasury of Enid Blyton Bedtime Stories

This edition first published in the United Kingdom in 2000 by
Brockhampton Press
20 Bloomsbury Street
London WC1B 3QA
an Imprint of the Caxton Publishing Group

© Text copyright, Enid Blyton Limited
© Illustration copyright, Hodder and Stoughton Limited

Designed and produced for Brockhampton Press by
Open Door Limited
80 High Street, Colsterworth, Lincolnshire NG33 5JA

Colour separation: GA Graphics Stamford

Title: Treasury of Enid Blyton Bedtime Stories
ISBN: 1-84186-067-0

Treasury of Enid Blyton Bedtime Stories

BROCKHAMPTON PRESS

Contents

Treasury of Enid Blyton Bedtime Stories
CHAPTER 1

Treasury of Enid Blyton Bedtime Stories

CHAPTER 1

Treasury of
Enid Blyton
Bedtime Stories
CHAPTER 2

Treasury of Enid Blyton Bedtime Stories
CHAPTER 2

Treasury of Enid Blyton Bedtime Stories
CHAPTER 3

Treasury of Enid Blyton Bedtime Stories
CHAPTER 3

Chapter 1

A Spell for a Puppy

There was once a little girl called Joan. She had a great many toys, books and games – almost every one you could think of. You might have thought she would be happy with so many, but she wasn't.

She hadn't the one thing that she really did badly want – and that was a real, live puppy! Her mother didn't like dogs in the house, and would never let her have a puppy, or a kitten either.

"Why do you keep saying you want a puppy to play with?" she often said impatiently to Joan. "You have so many lovely toys. What about your dolls' house? You never play with that now, Joan. Get it out this morning and give it a good clean. Take it out into the garden. It is nice and warm there, and it doesn't matter if you make a mess on the grass."

Joan didn't want to play with her dolls' house. She was not a little girl who was very fond of dolls. She liked running and jumping; she loved animals and birds. She wished she had been a boy. But she was obedient, so she fetched her dolls' house and took it out into the garden. She went down to the hedge at the bottom, where it was sheltered from the wind, for she did not want all the little carpets and curtains to blow away.

She took everything out and cleaned the house well with a wet cloth. She rubbed up the windows, and shook all the carpets. She polished the furniture and put it back again.

It was really a dear little house. There was a nice kitchen downstairs with a sink, and a fine drawing room and small dining room. Upstairs there was a little bathroom with a bath and a basin. Three bedrooms opened out of one another, all papered differently, each with their little carpet on the floor.

"It's a pity, I don't like this sort of toy as most little girls do," thought Joan, as she arranged all the furniture. "I wish I did. But people like different things, I suppose – and I do love animals – and I do wish I had one of my very own."

Just then the dinner-bell rang, and Joan went off to wash her hands and brush her hair. She stood the little house under the hedge out of the sun. She meant to go back after dinner and finish cleaning it outside. The front door knocker wanted a polish, and the chimney wanted washing.

But, after dinner, Mummy said she was going to take Joan out to tea, and the little girl was so pleased that she forgot all about the dolls' house out in the garden. She went off with her mother to catch the bus – and the little house was left under the hedge.

When Joan came back it was late and she was sent to bed at once. She snuggled down under the blankets – and then she suddenly remembered the dolls' house!

"Oh dear!" she said, sitting up in bed. "Whatever would Mummy say if she knew I had left my beautiful dolls' house out-of-doors? I really must go and get it!" She slipped on her dressing gown and went down the stairs. She went out of the garden door and ran down the path.

There was a bright moon and she could see everything quite clearly. She went to the hedge – and then she stopped still in the greatest surprise!

asleep in one of the small beds, a tiny pixie baby. It was really too good to be true. The little girl sighed with delight – and the pixies heard her!

They slammed the front door at once – and one of them opened a bedroom window and looked out.

"Who are you?" they cried to Joan.

"I'm the little girl this house belongs to," said Joan. "I've been cleaning it to-day, and I left it here and forgot it. What are you doing here?"

"Oh, we found it and thought it would do so nicely for us and our family," said the pixie, in a disappointed voice. "You

What do you think? There were lights in her little dolls' house – and people were walking about in the rooms – and the front door was wide open!

"Whoever is in there?" thought Joan, in great excitement. She bent down to see – and to her great delight she saw that the little folk inside were pixies with tiny wings. They were running about, talking at the tops of their voices. They sounded like swallows twittering.

Joan looked into one of the bedrooms through the window – and she saw, fast see, we lived in a nice hollow tree – but the woodmen came and cut it down – and we hadn't a home. Then we came along by your hedge and saw this lovely house. It's just the right size for us and, as there didn't seem to be anyone living in it, we thought we would take it."

"Well, I simply love to see you in it," said Joan. "I do really." "Would you let it to us?" asked the pixie. "We would pay you rent, if you liked."

"Oh, no," said Joan. "I don't want you to pay me for it. You can have it, if you like. I am very lucky to see you and talk to you, I think. I am most excited, really I am!"

"How kind of you to let us have it," said the pixie, beaming all over her little pointed face. "Can't we do something for you in return? Isn't there anything you want very much?"

"Well, yes, there is," said Joan. "I want a puppy dog very, very much. I have wanted one for years. But I have never had one."

"We'll give you a spell for one," said the pixie. She ran downstairs and opened the front door. She held up a very small box to Joan. "Take this," she said. "There is a spell inside. Blow it out of your window to-night and say 'Puppy, puppy, come to me. Make me happy as can be. Puppy, puppy, come to me!'"

"Oh, thank you!" said Joan, more excited than ever. "Listen, pixie. Don't you think I'd better take your house to the woods to-morrow? The gardener often comes here and he might be cross if he saw I'd left my house in the hedge."

"Yes, that's a good idea," said the pixie.

"We would like to be somewhere in the woods. Will you carry the house there to-morrow morning? We'll show you where we'd like it."

"Yes, I will," promised Joan. "Now, I must go. Good night, and thank you very much."

She ran off, looking back to see the little windows of her dolls' house lighted up so gaily. She went up to her bedroom and opened the small box. She took out the spell, which was like a tiny bit of thistledown, and blew it out of the window.

"Puppy, puppy, come to me. Make me happy as can be. Puppy, puppy, come to me!" she whispered.

Then she got into bed and fell fast asleep.

And whatever do you think happened next morning? Why, her Uncle Joe came to stay, and with him he brought a small, fat brown puppy in a basket – a present for Joan!

"Here you are!" he said to the delighted little girl. "I know you've always wanted a pup – and you shall have one! His name is Sandy – treat him well, and he'll be a good friend to you!"

Joan was full of joy. She loved the puppy, and it licked her nose and hands, pleased to have such a nice little mistress. She raced down the bottom of the garden with the puppy at her heels. The dolls' house was still there, and outside stood all the pixies, waiting for her to come.

"I've got my puppy, I've got my puppy!" she said, joyfully. "The spell worked! Now, I'll carry your house to the woods!"

She picked it up and carried it off, the pixies half flying, half running in front to show her the way. She put it down in a little glade by the side of a small stream and said good-bye once more. Then she and Sandy raced home again, a very happy pair.

And if you should happen to come across a dolls' house in the woods, don't touch it, will you? It will be the one belonging to the pixies! They still live there, you see!

Jinky's Joke

Once there was a wicked little pixie called Jinky. He was always playing jokes on people, and sometimes they were funny, but more often they were not.

One week he went to all the shops that sold pails and saucepans and ordered dozens to be sent to old Dame Cooky. Well, the poor old lady couldn't *imagine* why so many saucepans and pails kept arriving, and she really grew quite frightened when she saw her kitchen piled up from floor to roof with them. It took her two whole days to take them back to the shops and explain that she hadn't ordered them.

Another time, Jinky put glue on the big wooden seat that stood outside the town hall. People sat there and waited for the bus. Oh dear, how angry everyone was when the bus came by and they got up – because they left half their skirts behind them!

Now one day Jinky found a few tins of paint as he passed the builder's yard. He tucked them under his arm with a grin. He meant to borrow some of that paint.

He stole into Mother Creaky's back-garden and called her hens to him. He painted those poor hens with the paint out of the tins till they looked like feathered rainbows!

"Oh, Henny-Penny, you do look queer!" said Jinky, laughing as he set free a hen with a red beak, a yellow comb, a purple tail, green wings, and blue legs. And certainly the hen did look very strange. All the other hens looked at her, and then they ran at her and began to peck her, for they thought she was a stranger.

One by one, Jinky painted all the poor hens, and left them squabbling and pecking one another, for they couldn't bear to see such strange-looking creatures. Then Jinky heard Mother Creaky coming, and he hid behind the fence and watched.

"Oh! What's this I see?" cried Mother Creaky, in great astonishment, when she came to her gate. "Are these hens – or are they parrots or kingfishers? Never did I see such colours in my life!"

"Cluck, cluck, cluck!" said the hens sadly, and they ran to their mistress. They rubbed against her skirt and made it red, blue, green, orange, yellow, and purple.

"Oh, you poor creatures!" she cried. "Someone has painted you! You'll all have to be bathed."

Well, of course, hens hate the water, and Mother Creaky got pecked and scratched when she tried to get the paint off their feathers. She heard Jinky chuckling behind the fence, and caught sight of him running away. She was very angry.

"So that's Jinky again, is it?" she grumbled. "Well, it's time he got a fright. He left behind these paints – and I'll just go along to his house and do a little painting myself. I know he goes to supper with Higgle to-night. I shall have a nice time before he goes home."

So Mother Creaky picked up the tins of paint and went along to Jinky's cottage. The front door was black, with a letterbox and a knocker above it. Mother Creaky set to work.

She painted a big face! The letterbox was the mouth, and she painted that red. The knocker was the nose, and she painted that pink. She painted in big eyes and eyebrows and bright yellow hair and a witch's hat above it. When she had finished, it looked exactly like a witch's face looking down the path. Mother Creaky laughed and hid behind a bush.

The night came and the moon shone out brightly. Jinky came home, whistling, laughing whenever he thought of Mother Creaky's hens.

He turned in at his gate – and then he saw the painted face looking at him from his front door!

"Owwwwww!" cried Jinky in fright. "Ooooooh! Owwwwww! What is it? What is it?"

Then Mother Creaky spoke in a deep voice from behind her bush. It seemed to poor Jinky as if the face on his door were speaking, and he listened in fright.

"Jinky!" said the deep voice. "How dare you play tricks on my friend, Mother Creaky! How dare you upset poor Dame Cooky! I have come to punish you!"

"Oh, please don't, please don't!" wept Jinky. "I won't play tricks again. I didn't know that Dame Cooky and Mother Creaky had a witch for a friend. Please forgive me."

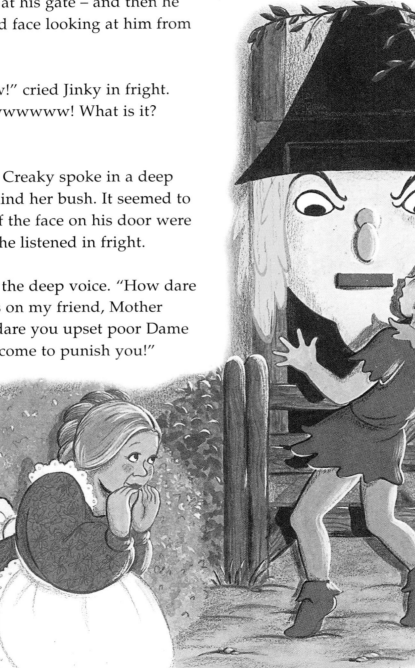

"I will only forgive you if you promise not to play unkind tricks any more," answered the deep voice.

"I promise, I promise!" sobbed Jinky, trembling so much that he could hardly stand.

"Very well. You may come into your house and I will not harm you," said the voice. But Jinky didn't dare to go in. No – he turned and fled away. He spent the night most uncomfortably in a dry ditch, with beetles and spiders crawling all over him.

And in the morning when he crept back to his house, his front door was just the same as usual! You see, Mother Creaky, with many giggles and chuckles, had washed away the witch's face with turpentine and water.

"He'll think twice before he plays a silly trick again," she said.

And Jinky did think twice. He didn't tell a single person about the witch he had seen – but Dame Creaky told the ice-cream man, and he told me – so that's how I know!

Visitors in the Night

The toys were very tired. They had had a very exciting day because the children had friends to tea – and all the toys had been played with.

"I simply can't keep my eyes open," said the pink cat. "It's no use. I must go to sleep."

"So must I," said the curly-haired doll. "I've been undressed and dressed so often today that I feel quite worn-out. I shall get into my cot and go to sleep."

And so, when somebody came into the playroom in the middle of the night, nobody was awake! The bear was giving tiny little snores in his corner, and the pink cat was all curled up in hers.

Somebody pattered in from a hole behind the cupboard, and squeaked loudly: "A message! I bring a message!"

Nobody answered. Nobody saw the small brown mouse with the twitching nose and long whiskers. He stood there in the middle of the floor, looking round in surprise.

"Isn't anyone awake? I bring a message. A MOST important message."

Still nobody woke up. The mouse looked for his best friend there – Clicky, the clockwork mouse. Ah, there he was. He ran over to him and pulled his tail hard.

"Clicky! Wake up! I've got a MESSAGE!"

Clicky woke up with a jump. "Dear me! What are you pulling my tail like that for?" he squealed.

"I've got a message from the five little fairies who live in Bluebell Wood," said the mouse, excitedly. "They came to a party given by the pixie who lives in our garden and, oh dear, they've fallen in the pond!"

"Goodness!" said the clockwork mouse. "Are they wet?"

"Yes, they're soaked through," said the real mouse. "And they sent me here with a message. Can the dolls' house dolls let them sleep in the dolls' house tonight? They simply *must* dry themselves, and get to bed, else they will have dreadful colds."

"I'll wake up the little dolls," said Clicky at once and soon he was knocking at the dolls' house door *rat-a-tat-a-tat*! The little mother-doll answered the door in her night-dress, most surprised.

When she heard about the wet fairies, she was quite upset. "The poor things! Mouse, go and bring them here at once. Are they small enough to come up your hole? They are? That's good. Then they will be small enough to sleep in the beds in my little dolls' house."

Off went the mouse at once, and the dolls' house dolls began to be very busy indeed. They ran water in the little bath – they put out clean towels – they made the beds and warmed blankets by the tiny kitchen fire. What excitement there was!

Soon five wet, miserable little fairies came trooping out of the mousehole with the mouse leading them. All the toys welcomed them, because Clicky had told them the news, of course. They were all awake now, and anxious to make the tiny fairies happy.

"It's so kind of you." Said Tippitty, the biggest fairy. "We're so wet and cold!"

The mother-doll welcomed them into the dolls' house at once. "A hot bath for you!" she said. "And warm beds. And we'll give you hot soup to drink when you're in bed. I'll dry your clothes while you're asleep."

The five fairies felt much better after a nice hot bath. They wiped themselves dry with the little towels, and then put on nighties belonging to the dolls' house dolls. They fitted them beautifully.

"Into bed with you," said the kind little mother-doll. "Now – here comes your soup!"

Soon the five fairies were drinking hot soup out of the tea-set cups. They felt warm and happy. How lucky they were to find a little house like this, with beds just the right size.

"We shan't get colds now," said Tippitty. "We shall feel quite all right in the morning. Oh, what a comfortable bed this is!"

Soon all five had snuggled down. The mother-doll tucked them up. "Please will you leave the light on?" asked Tippitty. "Just in case we wake up and have forgotten where we are!"

So the lights were left on in the little house – and the toys came creeping to the windows to peep in.

"Look – there they are, tucked up in the little dolls' beds," whispered the toy soldier. "Aren't they sweet?"

"They are just the right size," said the pink cat. "Aren't we lucky to have five fairies sleeping here tonight? It is a very great honour."

They crept back to the toy cupboard and fell asleep again. The dolls' house dolls went to sleep too. Everyone was really very tired.

They didn't wake up till quite late. One of the children came scampering in at eight o'clock, on her way down to breakfast. She stopped in surprise when she saw the dolls' house.

"Why! The lights are on!" she cried. "Jane! Come and see! Somebody has left the dolls' house lights on!"

Jane came running in too. "Goodness, Eileen – who could have left them on?" she said. "I know we turned them off last night. Let's look inside and see if anything has gone wrong with them."

Good gracious me! What a to-do there was in the dolls' house when the dolls heard the children outside! The mother-doll woke the five fairies at once.

"Quick! You must dress and go," she said. "The children are here – they may catch you and take you to school to show their friends!"

But there wasn't time to dress – Jane and Eileen were looking through the windows – and they saw the five fairies hopping out of bed in a hurry.

They stared as if they couldn't believe their eyes. Then they ran to their mother's room. "Mummy! Mummy, do come! There are fairies in our dolls' house! Come quickly. They're the prettiest things you ever saw!"

But when their mother came to the playroom and went to look in at the windows, there were no fairies to be seen!

They had caught up their clothes, fled down the little dolls' house stairs, run across the floor, and disappeared down the mousehole at top speed. Tippitty fell over her night-dress, but picked herself up just in time.

"Oh! There's nobody here now!" said Jane in dismay.

"There never was," said Mummy, laughing. "It was just a joke of yours."

"It wasn't!" said Eileen. "And look, the front door is open now – and see, one of the fairies has dropped a little petticoat as she ran! Oh, what a pretty, cobwebby thing!"

She showed her mother the tiny petticoat. Tippitty had dropped it without knowing.

"Well – it's a most extraordinary thing – and I don't really believe it!" said Mummy. "Now, do come and have your breakfast. Bring the tiny petticoat to show Daddy, if you like – but he won't believe your tale either."

He didn't, of course – but he would have if he had peeped in at the playroom the next night, and had seen five small fairies tripping out of the mousehole with parcels under their arms – the night-dresses belonging to the dolls' house dolls, all beautifully washed and ironed!

"Thank you for your help last night," said Tippitty. "And here are the night-dresses you lent us – and also a little magic spell in a box. It will grant you any wish you like – but only one – so think carefully before you use it!"

Well, what a surprise – a magic wish of their own! They simply can't wait to use it – and I really do wonder what they will wish for, don't you?

Thirteen O'clock

Once upon a time Sandy was walking home from school when he saw an extra fine dandelion clock.

"What a beauty!" he said, picking it with its stalk. "I wonder if it will tell me the right time."

He blew it – puff! A cloud of white fluffy seeds flew away. There were plenty left on the clock. He blew again – puff! More fluff flew away on the breeze. Puff! Puff! Puff! He counted as he blew.

"One o'clock! Two o'clock! Three! Four! Five! Six o'clock! Seven! Eight! Nine! Ten! Eleven o'clock! Twelve o'clock! *Thirteen o'clock!*"

At the thirteenth puff there was no fluff left on the dandelion clock at all. It was just an empty stalk.

And then things began to happen. A noise of little voices was heard, and Sandy looked down at his feet. Round him was a crowd of pixies, shouting loudly.

"Did you say thirteen o'clock? Hi, did you say thirteen o'clock?"

"Yes" said Sandy, in aston-ishment. "The dandelion clock said thirteen o'clock."

"Oh my goodness me, thirteen o'clock only happens once in a blue moon!" cried the biggest pixie. "Whatever shall we do?"

"Why, what's the matter?" asked Sandy. "What are you so upset about?"

"Don't you know?" shouted all the pixies together. "Why, at thirteen o'clock all the witches from Witchland fly on broomsticks, and if they see any elf, pixie, brownie or gnome out of Fairyland they catch them and take them away. Oh dear, goodness gracious, whatever shall we do?"

Sandy felt quite alarmed. "Do they take little boys, too?" he asked.

"We don't know, but they might," answered the biggest pixie. "Hark! Can you hear the Witches' Wind blowing?"

Sandy listened. Yes, a wind was blowing up, and it sounded a funny sort of wind, all whispery and strange.

"That's the wind the witches use to blow their broomsticks along," said the pixies. "Little boy, you'd better run home quickly."

But Sandy wasn't going to leave the little pixies alone. They were frightened, so he felt he must stay and look after them. "I'll stay with you," he said. "But do you think you could make me as small as you, because if I'm as big as this the witches will see me easily and catch me."

"That's easy to do," said the biggest pixie. "Shut your eyes, put your hands over your ears and whisper 'Hoona-looki-allo-pie' three times to yourself. Then you'll be as small as we are. When you want to get big again do exactly the same, but say the magic words backwards."

Sandy felt excited. He shut his eyes and covered his ears with his hands. Then he whispered the magic words three times – and lo and behold, when he opened his eyes again he was as small as the pixies! They crowded round him, laughing and talking.

"I am Gobbo," said the biggest one, "and this is my friend, Twinkle."

Sandy solemnly shook hands with Gobbo and Twinkle. Then, as the wind grew louder, the pixies crowded together in alarm, and looked up at the sky.

"Where shall we go to hide?" said Twinkle. "Oh, quick, think of somewhere, somebody, or the witches will be along and will take us prisoners!"

Everybody thought hard, and then Sandy had a good idea.

"As I came along I noticed an old saucepan thrown away in the hedge," he said. "Let's go and find it and get under it. It will hide us all beautifully."

Off went all the pixies, following Sandy. He soon found the saucepan, and by pushing hard they managed to turn it upside-down over them, so that it quite hid them. There was a hole in the side out of which they could peep. "I've dropped my handkerchief," suddenly cried Twinkle, pointing to where a little red hanky lay on the ground some way off. "I must go and get it."

"No, don't," said Gobbo. "You'll be caught. The witches will be along any minute now. Hark how the wind is blowing!"

"But I must get it!" cried Twinkle. "If I don't the witches will catch sight of it out there, and down they'll all come to see what it is. Then they'll sniff pixies nearby and come hunting under this saucepan for us."

"Oooooooooh!" groaned all the pixies, in fright. "Well, go and get it quickly!" said Gobbo to Twinkle. "Hurry up!"

Twinkle crept out from under the saucepan and everybody watched him anxiously. The wind grew louder and louder and all the tall grasses

swayed like trees in the wind. Then there came a sort of voice in the wind and Sandy listened to hear what it said.

"The witches are coming, the witches are coming!" it said, in a deep-down, grumbling sort of voice, rushing into every hole and corner. Sandy peeped through the hole in the saucepan to see what Twinkle was doing. He was dodging here and there between the grasses. At last he reached the place where his red handkerchief lay, and he picked it up and put it into his pocket.

And then, oh my goodness, the pixies in the saucepan saw the first witches coming! They shouted to Twinkle, and he looked up in the sky. There they were, three witches in pointed hats and long cloaks, sitting on long broomsticks, flying through the cloudy sky.

"Quick, Twinkle, quick!" yelled Sandy and the pixies. How they hoped the witches wouldn't see him! He crouched down under a yellow buttercup till they were past, and then began to run to the saucepan.

"There are two more witches coming!" shouted the pixies, pointing. Sure enough, two more could be seen in the windy sky, much lower down than the others. Twinkle crept under a green stinging-nettle and stayed there without movement till the witches had gone safely by.

"Poor Twinkle! He *will* be stung!" said Gobbo, sadly. When the two witches were past Twinkle ran from beneath the nettle straight to the saucepan and crept underneath in safety. How glad all the pixies were! They crowded round him and stroked his nettle-stung hands and face.

"Never mind, Twinkle, you're safe here," they said.

"Look at all the witches now!" cried Sandy peeping through the hole. "Oh my! What a wonderful sight! I'm glad I'm seeing this."

It certainly was a marvellous sight! The sky was simply full of flying witches, and some of them had black cats sitting in front of them on the broomsticks. The cats coiled their tails round the sticks and held on like monkeys. It was funny to see them.

"Does this always happen at thirteen o'clock?" asked Sandy.

"Always," said Twinkle, solemnly. "But thirteen o'clock only happens once in a blue moon, as I told you before. The moon must have been blue this month. Did you notice it?"

"Well, no, I didn't," said Sandy. "I'm nearly always in bed when it's moonlight. Oh I say! Look! One of the witches has lost her black cat!"

The pixies peeped out of the hole in the saucepan. Sure enough, one of the black cats had tumbled off its broomstick. It had tried to be clever and wash itself on the broomstick, and had lost its hold and tumbled off. It was falling through the air, and the witch was darting down with her broomstick, trying her best to catch it.

She just managed to grab hold of the cat before it fell on the ground – but her broomstick was smashed to pieces, and the witch rolled over and over on the grass, holding the cat safely in her arms. She sat up and looked round. When she saw her broken broomstick she began to howl.

"It's broken. It's broken! I'll never be able to fly back home! Boo hoo hoo!"

Sandy was frightened to see the witch rolling over and over. He thought she would be sure to hurt herself. He was a very kind-hearted boy, and he longed to go and ask her if she was all right. He began to squeeze himself under the saucepan, meaning to go and see if the witch was hurt. But the pixies tried to pull him back.

"Don't go, don't go," they whispered, for the witch was quite near. "She'll change you into a black-beetle."

"Why should she?" asked Sandy. "I'm going to be kind to her. Besides, she's got a nice face, rather like my granny's – I'm sure she isn't a bad witch."

He wriggled himself away from the hands of the pixies and ran over to the witch. She was sitting down on the grass crying big tears all down her cheeks. The cat was on her lap, still looking frightened.

The witch was most surprised to see him. Sandy stopped just by her. She had a very tall pointed hat, a long cloak round her shoulders, with silver suns, moons and stars all over it. The cat arched its back and spat angrily at the little boy.

"Excuse me," said Sandy, politely. "I saw you roll over on the ground when your broomstick broke, and I came to see if you were hurt."

"Well," said the witch, holding out her left hand, "I'm not much hurt – but my hand is a bit cut. I must have hit it against a stone when I rolled over."

"I'll tie it up for you with my handkerchief." Said Sandy. "It's quite clean."

The witch looked more astonished than ever. She held out her hand and Sandy tied it up very neatly.

"Thank you," said the witch. "That's most kind of you. Oh dear – just look at my poor broomstick – it's broken in half! I shall never get back to Witchland again!"

Sandy looked at the broomstick. The broom part was all right, but the stick was broken. Sandy felt in his pocket to see if he had brought his knife with him. Yes, he had!

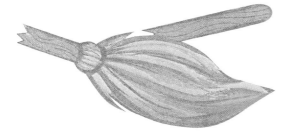

"I'll cut you another stick from the hedge," he said. "Then you can fit it into the broomhead and use it to fly away with!"

"You're the cleverest, kindest boy I ever met!" said the witch. "Thank you so much! Most people are afraid of witches, you know, because they think we will change them into black-beetles, or something – but that's an old-fashioned idea. The old witches *were* like that but nowadays we witches are decent folk, making magic spells that will do no-one any harm at all."

"Well, I'm glad to hear *that*!" said Sandy, hoping that the pixies under the saucepan were hearing it, too. He went to the hedge and cut another stick for the witch. He fitted it neatly into the broomhead and threw away the broken stick. The witch was very pleased.

She said a magic spell over it to make it able to fly. Then she turned to Sandy.

"Won't you have a ride with me?" she asked. "It is great fun. I will see that you are safe."

"Ooh, I'd *love* a ride!" cried Sandy, in delight. "But you are sure you won't take me away to Witchland?"

"I told you that witches don't do horrid things now," said the witch. "Do I *look* like a nasty witch?"

"No, you don't," said Sandy. "Well, I'll come for a ride – I'd love to! I'll be awfully late for my dinner but an adventure like this doesn't come often!'

He perched himself on the broomstick, behind the witch, who took her black cat on her knee. Just as they were about to set off, there came a great clatter, and the saucepan nearby was overturned by the pixies. They streamed out, shouting and calling.

"Take us for a ride, too! Take us for a ride, too!"

The witch looked at them in amazement. She had no idea that any pixies were near. She laughed when she saw where they had been hiding.

"Climb up on the stick," she said. "I'll give you a ride, too!"

Goodness, there wasn't room to put a blade of grass on that broomstick after all the pixies had climbed up on it! What a squash there was, to be sure!

The witch called out a string of magic words and the broomstick suddenly flew up into the air with a jerk. Sandy held on tightly. The pixies yelled in delight and began to sing joyfully. All the other witches flying high in the sky laughed to see such a crowded broomstick. Sandy did enjoy himself. He was very high up, and the wind whistled in his ears and blew his hair straight back from his head.

"Now we're going down again!" said the witch, and the broomstick swooped downwards. It landed gently and all the pixies tumbled off in a heap. Sandy jumped off and thanked the witch very much for such a lovely ride.

"I must go now," she said. "The hour of thirteen o'clock is nearly over and I must return to Witchland. Good-bye, kind little boy, and I'll give you another ride next time it's thirteen o'clock. If you wait for me here, I'll take you all the way to Witchland and back!"

Off she went, she and her black cat, and left Sandy standing on the grass, watching her fly away. The pixies waved to the witch and she waved back. "Well, that *was* an adventure!" cried the pixies. "We'll never be afraid of witches again, that's certain! Hooray!"

"I wonder what the time is," said Sandy. "What comes after thirteen o'clock? Is it fourteen o'clock?"

"Oh no!" said Twinkle. "Thirteen o'clock just comes and goes. It isn't any time really. It always comes after twelve o'clock, but it's followed by one o'clock as if nothing had happened in between!"

Somewhere a church clock chimed the hour. Sandy listened. Then the clock struck one, and no more.

"One o'clock, one o'clock!" cried the pixies their voices growing very small and faint. "Thirteen o'clock is over! Good-bye, good-bye!"

Sandy looked at them – they were vanishing like the mist, and in a moment or two he could see nothing of them. They just weren't there.

"I must make myself big again," he thought. He remembered the words quite well. He shut his eyes and covered up his ears. He had to say the magic words backwards, so he thought hard before he spoke.

"Pie-allo-looki-hoona!" he said. When he opened his eyes he was his own size again! He set off home, running as fast as he could, for he was afraid that his mother would be wondering where he was.

He ran into the house and found his mother just putting out his dinner. She didn't seem to think he was late at all!

"You're just in nice time," she said to Sandy. "Good boy! You must have come straight from school without stopping!"

"But mother – ever such a lot has happened since I left school," said Sandy in surprise. "I'm dreadfully late!"

"No, darling, it's only just gone one o'clock," said his mother, looking at the clock.

"Didn't *you* have thirteen o'clock, too, this morning?" asked Sandy, sitting down to his dinner.

"What *are* you talking about?" said his mother with a laugh. "Thirteen o'clock! Whoever heard of that? That only happens in Fairyland, once in a blue moon, I should think!"

Sandy thought about it. Perhaps it was true – perhaps thirteen o'clock belonged to the fairies, and not to the world of boys and girls. How lucky he had been to have that one magic hour of thirteen o'clock with the pixies and the witch. And next time it was thirteen o'clock he was going to ride on a broomstick again. Oh, what fun!

"I do hope it will be thirteen o'clock again soon," he said.

"Eat up your dinner and don't talk nonsense!" said his mother, laughing.

But it wasn't nonsense, was it? Sandy is going to blow all the dandelion clocks he sees so that he will know when it is thirteen o'clock again. If you blow them too, you may find that magic hour as well!

The Little Musical Box

In the playroom was a dear little musical box. It was quite round, and it had a handle that could be turned. When you turned the handle, the music played.

"Tiddley-iddley-oh-lee-oh," went the music, and the toys danced to it night after night.

"It's funny to think that music is shut up in this box, isn't it?" said the little doll in the blue dress. "I do like it."

The goldfish in the big glass bowl up on the window-sill tapped a nose against the glass. That meant that he wanted to speak to the toys. So the toy soldier climbed up to listen.

"Bring the music up here," said the goldfish, in his bubbly voice. "I want to hear it too."

So the toy soldier and the teddy carried the little round box carefully up to the goldfish bowl. The bear turned the handle and the music played merrily. "Tiddley-idd-ley, oh-lee-oh!" "Oh, it's lovely!" said the goldfish and he waved his tail about in time to the music. "Please do sometimes bring it to the window-sill for me to hear."

The toys never played the music until it was night-time, and the three children were in bed. They loved Freda, Mollie and John, and were always excited when they came to play with them. But when they were in bed and asleep it would never do to make a noise and wake them up.

The toy soldier always pushed the door almost shut when they played the musical box at night, or raced round the floor in the little clockwork engine. They really had fun then, especially if the engine-driver was in a good temper and

let some of them drive the engine themselves.

One night, when the toys were playing together, there came a great wind that blew outside, and made the trees sway and bend. "Listen to that!" said the bear. "What a noise!"

"I can hear the rain on the window now," said the little black doll. "Drip-drip-drip, drop-drop-drop!"

"And I can feel it!" said the toy soldier suddenly. "Goodness, where's my umbrella?"

"Don't be silly! The window is shut," said the bear.

"Well, it isn't – look, the wind has blown it open," said the black doll. "I can

feel the rain coming in too. And just see how the curtains are blowing!"

The wind had blown so hard that the window had been jerked wide open! It was swinging to and fro, and the curtains were flapping wildly.

The goldfish in his bowl up on the window-sill was frightened. He tapped on the glass with his nose. "The curtain is flapping against my bowl!" he said, in his little bubbling voice. "I'm afraid!"

"Goodness! I hope the curtains don't overturn his bowl!" said the toy soldier – and do you know, just as he had said that, the wind blew the curtains so hard that they pushed the goldfish bowl right over!

Crash! It tipped on its side and all the water poured out of it in a rush, splashing down the wall to the floor below.

"The goldfish! He's been tipped out too!" cried the black doll. "Oh, Goldie! Are you hurt?"

The little fish was flapping about on the carpet, panting for breath. "I can't breathe when I'm out of water!" he said. "Water! Put me in water! Quick!"

But there wasn't any water to put him in. There wasn't even a vase of flowers he could be slipped into! The toys were in a terrible worry about him.

"He can't breathe! Water, water!" cried the bear. But it wasn't a bit of good shouting out for water. The bathroom was a long way away and water didn't come by itself!

"We'll carry him to the bathroom!" said the doll in the blue dress. "Perhaps there is some water in the bath."

But, you know, the goldfish was so very slippery that nobody could hold him. He just slipped out of their hands, and flapped back on to the carpet again.

And then the toy soldier had a wonderful idea. "Where's the musical box? Let's carry it into the children's bedroom and play it as fast as we can!"

"Oh yes – then they'll wake up and come and see what's happening!" cried the bear. "They'll see poor old Goldie!"

The toy soldier and the bear took hold of the musical box and carried it out of the door, down the passage and in at the door of the children's bedroom. It felt very heavy to them, because they weren't very big.

They put it down on the bedroom floor with a bump. "Now!" said the bear, and he took hold of the handle. He turned it quickly and the music came tinkling out, loud and clear and sweet.

"Tiddley-iddley-oh-lee-oh! Tiddley-iddley-oh-lee-oh!" The musical box played its little tune on and on, and the toy soldier and bear took turns at winding the handle round and round.

Freda woke up first. She sat up, surprised. "Why – it sounds like the musical box!" she said, and she woke up John and Mollie. They sat up and heard it too.

Mollie switched on her torch – and there, in its light, she saw the bear and the toy soldier with the musical box, playing it without stopping!

"Look! Oh look! It's Teddy and the toy soldier with our musical box!" cried Mollie. "Why have they brought it here?"

Just as she said that, the toy soldier and Teddy lifted the musical box and hurried out of the room, hoping the children would follow them to the playroom.

They did, of course – and the very first thing they saw was poor old Goldie flapping very feebly on the floor. He was in a very bad way now, and the children had only just come in time.

"Goldie! You're out of your bowl! Oh look – the wind blew the window open, and the curtains must have knocked over the bowl!" cried John.

Mollie took the bowl and ran to the bathroom. She filled it with water and ran back. John picked up poor Goldie very gently and slid him into the bowl.

He flapped feebly and turned on his side. The children and the toys watched him, hardly daring to breathe. Would Goldie be all right?"

He turned the right way up again. He moved his fins more strongly. His mouth opened and shut as he took in the water he had missed so much. He gasped a few words in his little bubbly voice. "Thank you! I'll be all right now!"

"Well!" said Freda, in surprise, looking round at the toys, "WHO had the bright idea of waking us up with the musical box so that we could save poor Goldie? You are very good, clever toys – and tomorrow we will give a party for you, just to show you how grateful we are!"

They shut the window tightly so that the wet curtains hung still and straight. The bowl would not be knocked over again!

"Good night," said the children, and went back to bed – and in the morning they wondered if they had dreamed it all!

"No – we couldn't have," said John. "We couldn't possibly all dream the same dream. Anyway – if it's really true we'll find the carpet wet, where the water was spilt from Goldie's bowl last night."

It *was* wet, of course, so they knew it had all really happened. And now they are giving a grand party for the toys!

Real biscuits! Real lemonade poured out of the teapot! Real bits of chocolate! Well – the toys had never enjoyed a party so much before.

Just look at them, having a good time – and even Goldie isn't forgotten. The toy soldier is dropping a bit of biscuit into his bowl!

The Dumpy Wizard's Party

The Dumpy Wizard was just like his name – fat and round and dumpy. He was a nice old fellow, as merry as a blackbird, and he simply loved giving parties.

People loved going to his parties too! They were so jolly – always lots of nice things to eat and exciting games to play.

But the Dumpy Wizard was very particular about the people he invited to his parties. He wouldn't have anyone greedy. So, if someone was left out of one of his parties, people always knew there was something wrong with them just then.

Now one day Tricky the gnome was running down the street, and he turned the corner quickly. Bump! He banged right into Dumpy the Wizard, and they both fell over. Dumpy sat in a puddle. Tricky banged his head against a wall.

"What did you do that for?" roared Dumpy.

"What do you mean?" yelled back Tricky. "You bumped into me as much as I bumped into you!"

"Why don't you look where you are going?" shouted Dumpy.

"I was, but you came where I was just about to go!" cried Tricky.

"Don't be silly," said Dumpy, drying himself with his handkerchief.

"I'm not," said Tricky.

"Oh yes, you are!" said Dumpy.

"Oh no, I'm not!" said Tricky.

"Oh yes, you are!" said Dumpy. "I shan't ask you to my next party."

"I shall come all the same – yes, and eat up your nicest jellies!" said Tricky.

"You won't," said Dumpy.

"Oh yes, I will," said Tricky.

"Oh no, you won't," said Dumpy.

"Now then, move on, you two," said Blueboy, the policeman of the village. "Stop quarrelling!"

So Tricky and Dumpy had to move on. Dumpy was quite sure he *wouldn't* let Tricky come to his party – and Tricky was quite sure he *would* go – and eat up the best jellies too!

Dumpy sent out his invitations – and do you know, everyone was invited this time – except Tricky, of course! He said he didn't care, not he! And in his cunning little head he made a plan.

It was to be a fine party. There was to be a gramophone going, and everyone was to sing and dance to it. There were to be four different coloured jellies – green, red, orange and pink – and a fine cake with a rabbit in sugar on the top. Ooooh!

The day soon came. Everyone put on his best clothes and looked as excited as could be. Only Tricky kept on his old clothes, but he didn't seem to care one bit – he just ran about as usual, humming and whistling as if *he* didn't care about parties.

Four o'clock came. Gnomes, goblins, brownies, and pixies crowded into Dumpy's little cottage. Only two people were not there – Tricky, of course – and Blueboy the policeman, who had to guard everyone's house because they were all empty.

The gramophone was set going. The dancing began. People sang as they danced. What a noise there was! Everyone was excited and happy, because, set out at the end of the room, was a table full of good things. The four coloured jellies shivered and shook. The sugar rabbit on the iced cake stood up and looked with very sugary eyes at all the dancers. It was a very merry evening.

Just as everyone was feeling hungry, and thinking it was about time the dancing stopped and the eating began, there came a knock at Dumpy's front door.

Blim-blam!

"Who can that be?" said Dumpy, in surprise.

He opened the door. Outside stood someone dressed in a blue uniform, looking very stern.

"Hallo, Blueboy," said Dumpy, in surprise. "What do you want?"

"Have you any idea of the noise you are making?" said Blueboy, in a stern voice.

"Oh, we are only dancing and singing," said Dumpy. "We are not making much noise, Blueboy."

"And I say you *are*!" said Blueboy. "I could hear it very plainly indeed from outside. You may not be able to hear what the noise is like from inside. It sounds really *dreadful* out here! You will wake everyone up!"

"But there is nobody to wake up," said Dumpy. "Everyone is here."

"Don't argue with me, Dumpy," said Blueboy, in such a cross voice that Dumpy was quite surprised. "I tell you that the noise from outside is simply dreadful."

He emptied the four lovely jellies into his helmet, and snatched the sugar rabbit off the cake. Then he slipped quietly out of the kitchen door and ran out of the back garden, home! He had been to the party after all!

The people outside crowded together and listened to hear the dreadful noise that Dumpy's party was supposed to have been making. They listened – and they listened.

"I can't hear a sound!" said Gobbo the pixie.

"Not a word!" said Tippy the gnome.

"I'll come out and hear it," said Dumpy. He turned round and called to his guests. "The policeman says that the noise we are making sounds simply dreadful outside I'm going to hear it."

"You'd better *all* come and hear it!" said the policeman. "Then you will believe what I say. Come along, everyone!"

Blueboy went into the house and pushed everyone out. He shut the door – and once the door was shut, he took off his big helmet – and he wasn't Blueboy at all! He was naughty Tricky, who had dressed up as a policeman to play a joke on Dumpy!

"The party isn't a bit noisy!" said Dumpy crossly. "I don't know what Blueboy meant. Why, there might be nobody in the house, it's so quiet! There's not a sound to be heard!"

"Well," said Happy the goblin, with a chuckle. "There *is* nobody in the house now – except Blueboy! We've all come out – to listen to ourselves making a noise indoors! Ho, ho, ho!"

"Ho, ho, ho!" roared everyone – and really, it *was* very funny, wasn't it! They had all gone outside to listen to the dreadful noise they were making *in*side! Dear, dear, dear, whatever next!

"Come on in," said Dumpy. "We'll tell that silly old Blueboy we didn't hear a sound!"

So into the house they all went – but where was Blueboy? Nowhere to be found! And where were the four beautiful jellies? Nowhere to be seen! And where, oh, where was that lovely sugar rabbit? He was gone – and the kitchen door was wide open! Oh dear!

"That wasn't Blueboy, it was Tricky!" suddenly cried Dumpy. "Yes, it was. I thought his voice wasn't Blueboy's. Oh, he has been to my party, as he said he would – and taken the best jellies – and my beautiful sugar rabbit too!"

"All because we were foolish enough to do what he told us – and leave the house to hear the noise we were making!" groaned Happy the goblin. "I know, Dumpy, let me run to Tricky's cottage and tell him we've found out his trick – and it was really very funny, you know – and say he can come to the party if he brings back the jellies and the sugar rabbit."

53

The Dumpy Wizard's Party

"All right," said Dumpy. "Go and tell him. He is too clever for me – I'd rather he was my friend than my enemy! Goodness knows what he would make us do next!"

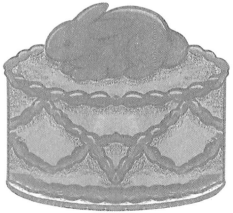

So Happy raced off to Tricky's cottage. Tricky had emptied the jellies out of his helmet on to a big dish and was just going to eat them.

"Hi, stop!" said Happy, running in. "We want you to come to the party. That was a

clever trick you played, Tricky – but don't make Dumpy unhappy about his jellies and sugar rabbit. He was very proud of them!"

"Very well," said Tricky, getting up. "I'll come – and I'll bring the jellies and the rabbit with me!"

So back he went to the party with Happy – and everyone laughed and said he was a rascal, and Dumpy said he would forgive him if he wouldn't play any more tricks.

So they all settled down again, and the gramophone played, and the jellies were eaten, and the sugar rabbit was put back on the cake, where he looked simply splendid.

"It was a lovely party – even if the jellies *did* taste a bit helmety," said Tricky, when he said good-bye to Dumpy.

"Well – that was *your* fault!" said Dumpy with a grin.

Jinky the Jumping Frog

Jinky was a little green jumping frog who lived in the toy cupboard with all the other toys. He had a spring inside him that made him able to jump high up in the air, and he often frightened the toys with his enormous jumps. He didn't *mean* to frighten them, but, you see, he couldn't walk or run, so his only way of getting about was to jump.

"I'm sorry if I startle you," he said to the angry toys. "Please try and get used to my big hops. I can't do anything else, you see."

The toys thought he was silly. He was a shy little frog, and he didn't say much, so the toys thought him stupid. They left him out of all their games at night, and he was often very lonely when he sat in a corner of the toy cupboard and watched the toys playing with one of the nursery balls.

Now the prettiest and daintiest of all the toys was Silvertoes, the fairy doll. She was perfectly lovely, and she had a silver crown on her head, a frock of finest gauze that stood out all round her, a pair of shining silver wings, and a little silver wand, which she always carried in her right hand. Everyone loved her, and the green frog loved her most of all.

But she wouldn't even look at him! He had once made her jump by hopping suddenly down by her, and she had never forgiven him. So Jinky watched her from a distance and wished and wished she would smile at him just once. But she never did.

One night there was a bright moon outside, and the brownie who lived inside the apple tree just by the nursery window came and called the toys.

"Let's all go out into the garden and dance in the moonlight," he said. "It's lovely and warm, and we could have a fine time together."

Out went all the toys through the window! They climbed down the apple tree, and slid to the grass below. Then they began to dance in the moonlight. They all took partners except the green frog, who was left out. He sat patiently on the grass, watching the other toys, and wishing that he could dance too.

There was such a noise of talking and laughing that no-one noticed a strange throbbing sound up in the sky. No-one, that is, except the green frog. He heard it and he looked up. He saw a bright silver aeroplane, about as big as a rook, circling round and round above the lawn.

Then someone looked down from the aeroplane and Jinky shivered with fright – for who should it be but Sly-one, the gnome who lived in Bracken Country, far away. He was a sly and unpleasant person, and nobody, fairy or toy, liked to have anything to do with him.

"I wonder what he wants to come here for to-night!" said Jinky to himself. "He's up to some mischief, I'm sure!"

He was! He suddenly swooped down in his aeroplane, landed near the toys, ran up to the fairy doll, snatched her away from the teddy bear who was dancing with her, and ran off with her to his aeroplane!

How she screamed! "Help! Help! Oh, please save me, toys!"

The gnome felt quite safe in the air. He circled round and round the toys and bent over the side of his aeroplane to laugh at them.

"Ha, ha!" he said. "Put me in prison, did you say? Well, come and catch me!"

To the great anger of the toys he flew very low indeed, just above their heads. The teddy bear, who was tall, tried to jump up and hang on to the aeroplane, but he couldn't quite reach it. He was in despair.

The toys were so astonished that they stood and gaped at the bold gnome. He threw the fairy doll into his aeroplane, jumped in himself, and away he went into the air! Then the toys suddenly saw what was happening, and began to shout.

"You wicked gnome! Bring her back at once! We'll put you in prison if you don't!"

"Whatever shall we do?" he cried to the toys. "We can't possibly rescue the fairy doll in that horrid aeroplane."

"Ha, ha!" laughed the gnome again, swooping down to the toys – and just at that moment the green frog saw his chance! He would do a most ENORMOUS jump and see if he could leap right on to the aeroplane.

He jumped. My goodness me, what a leap that was! You should have seen him! He jumped right up into the air, and reached out his front feet for the aeroplane. And he just managed it! He hung on the tail of the plane, and then managed to scramble up. The gnome had not seen him.

The toys were too astonished to say a word. They stood with open mouths looking up at the brave green frog, and he signed to them to say nothing about him. He thought that if the gnome did not know he was there he might be able to rescue the fairy doll without much difficulty.

The gnome flew off in his aeroplane. He wanted to reach Bracken Cottage that night, and he meant to marry the fairy doll in the morning. He thought it would be lovely to have such a pretty creature cooking his dinner and mending his clothes.

The frog crouched down on the tail of the aeroplane. It was very cold there, but he didn't mind. He was simply delighted to think that he would have a chance to do something for the pretty fairy doll.

At last Sly-One arrived at Bracken Cottage. He glided down and landed in the big field at the back of his house. Out he jumped, and turned to the fairy doll, who was cold, frightened and miserable.

"Wait here a minute and I'll just go and unlock the door," he said. "Then I'll come back and fetch you." He ran off – and as soon as he had gone the green frog hopped down into the seat beside the fairy doll.

She nearly screamed with fright, but he stopped her. "Sh!" he said. "It's only me, Jinky the jumping frog. I've come to save you. Do you think we can fly back in this aeroplane?"

"Oh, Jinky, I'm so glad to see you," sobbed the poor doll. "Look, you jerk that handle up, and the aeroplane should fly up into the air."

Jinky jerked the handle in front of him, but nothing happened. The gnome had stopped the engine and, of course, it wouldn't move. Jinky was in despair. He didn't in the least know how to fly the plane, and he was terribly afraid that if it did begin to fly there would be an accident.

"It's no good," he said, hopping out of the seat. "I can't make it go. Come on, fairy doll, get out, and jump on my back. I'll leap off with you, and perhaps we can escape that way."

"Take the handle out of the aeroplane," said the doll. "Then the nasty gnome can't fly after us in it. He won't be able to make it go up!"

"Good idea!" said the frog, and he tore off the handle. He put it into his mouth, for he was afraid to throw it anywhere in case the gnome found it again. He thought he would carry it a little way and then throw it into a bush. The fairy doll climbed on to his back, and held tight.

"Now please, don't be frightened," said the jumping frog. "I shall jump high, but you will be quite safe. I can't walk or run, you know."

"*I* shan't be frightened," said the fairy doll, clinging to his back. "I think you are the dearest, bravest, handsomest, strongest frog that I ever saw!"

"Well! How Jinky swelled with pride when he heard that! He looked behind him to see that the gnome was still far away – but, oh my goodness, he was running back from his cottage at top speed, for he had seen the doll get out of the aeroplane!

Jinky wasted no time but leapt high into the air and down again. Again and again he jumped, and each jump took him further away from the gnome, who had gone to his aeroplane to fly after them.

When he found that the starting handle had gone, he was very angry. He jumped out of the plane and ran to his garage. He opened the doors, and in a few moments Jinky heard the sound of a car engine roaring.

"Oh, my!" he thought in dismay. "If he comes after me in the car I shan't have any chance at all!"

On he went, leaping as far as he could each time. The fairy doll clung to him, and called to him to go faster still. Behind them came the gnome's car, driven at a fearful speed.

Then, crash! There came a tremendous noise, and Jinky turned round to see what had happened. The gnome had driven so fast round a corner that he had gone smash into a tree, and his car was broken to pieces. Sly-One jumped out unhurt, very angry indeed. He shook his fist at the jumping frog, and looked at his broken car. Then he ran to a cottage nearby and thumped at the door.

The sleepy gnome came, and asked him what he wanted.

"Lend me your bicycle," demanded the gnome. "I want to chase a wicked frog."

The goblin brought it out and the gnome jumped into the saddle. Off he pedalled at a furious rate after the frog and the doll.

"He's got a bicycle now!" shouted the fairy doll to Jinky. "Oh, hurry up, hurry up!" Jinky jumped as fast as he could, but the doll was heavy and he began to be afraid that he would never escape. Behind him came the gnome on the bicycle, ringing his bell loudly all the time.

Suddenly the frog came to a village, and in the middle of the street stood a policeman with red wings. He held out his hand to stop Jinky and the doll, but with a tremendous jump the frog leapt right over him and was at the other end of the village before the angry policeman knew what had happened. Then he heard the loud ringing of Sly-One's bicycle bell, and turned to stop the gnome. He held out his hand sternly.

But the gnome couldn't and wouldn't stop! He ran right into the astonished policeman, and knocked him flat on his face. Bump! The gnome flew off his bicycle and landed right in the middle of the duck pond nearby. The bicycle ran off by itself and smashed against a wall.

How angry that policeman was! He jumped to his feet and marched over to the gnome. "I arrest you for not stopping when I told you to, and for knocking me down," he said.

But the gnome slipped away from him, and ran down the street after the doll and the frog. The policeman ran after him, and off went the two, helter-skelter down the road.

The frog had quite a good start by now, and he was leaping for all he was worth. The doll was telling him all that had happened, and when he heard how the gnome had run into the policeman, he laughed so much that he got a stitch in his side and had to stop to rest.

"Oh, don't laugh!" begged the doll. "It really isn't funny. Do get on Jinky."

His stitch was soon better, and on he went again, while some way behind him panted the gnome and the policeman.

The frog felt sure he could jump faster than the gnome could run, so he wasn't so worried as he had been. For two more hours he jumped and jumped, and at last he came to the place where the toys had been dancing last night. They had all gone back to the nursery, very sad because they felt sure that the fairy doll and the frog were lost forever.

The frog jumped in at the window, and the fairy doll slid off his back. How the toys shouted with glee! How they praised the brave frog, and begged his pardon for the unkind things they had said and done to him. And you should have seen his face when the fairy doll suddenly threw her arms round his neck and kissed him! He was so pleased that he jumped all round the room for joy.

Suddenly there was a shout outside. It was the gnome still running, and the policeman after him! The gnome was so angry that he meant to run into the nursery and fight the jumping frog!

Then teddy bear did a clever thing. He put an empty box just underneath the window, and waited by it with the lid in his hands. The gnome jumped through the window straight into the box, and the bear clapped the lid down on him!

When the policeman came into the room too, the bear bowed gravely to him and handed him the box neatly tied round with string.

"Here is your prisoner," he said. "Please take him away, he is making such a noise."

The surprised policeman thanked the bear, bowed to the toys, and went out of the window again. Then the toys sat down and had a good laugh, but the one who laughed the loudest of all was Jinky, the little green frog!

Enid Blyton

Grumph the Rocking Horse

Grumph was an enormous rocking-horse and he lived in the middle of the nursery floor. He was a fine fellow with black spots all over him, a big mane, and a bushy black tail.

He rocked to and fro and took children for long rides. They all loved him – but the toys were afraid of him.

Sometimes he would begin to rock when they were playing about, and then, how they ran out of the way!

"Be careful, be careful!" they would cry.

"Tell us before you rock, Grumph! You might rock on one of us and hurt us badly!"

Then Grumph would laugh and think it was a great joke to scare the toys so much.

"You are not kind," the teddy bear said to him. "One day you will be sorry, Grumph." And so he was, as you will hear.

It happened that Billy and Betty had been playing with their toys one afternoon, and had left them all about the nursery when they had gone to bed. Nurse saw them there and was cross. "Those children will have to clear them up to-morrow morning!" she said, and she left them on the floor.

Now, the toy soldier's head and one of his hands were just under the rocker of the rocking-horse. He was quite safe unless Grumph suddenly rocked. The toys all watched anxiously, waiting for midnight to come so that they might rush out to the toy soldier and pull him out of danger.

Grumph chose that night to give the toys a scare. As soon as twelve o'clock began to strike, and he knew it was midnight, when all toys can come alive, Grumph began to rock.

"Stop! Stop!" shrieked the toys, running forward. "The toy soldier is underneath!"

But Grumph didn't listen. No, he thought the toys were scared as usual, and he didn't listen to what they said. To and fro he rocked – and the poor toy soldier was underneath!

Oh dear, oh dear, when the toys got to him, what a sight he was! His bearskin hat was all torn off, and his right hand was squashed to bits. The toys pulled him away and he began to cry.

"What's the matter?" asked Grumph, stopping and looking down.

"You wicked horse! We told you to stop! Now see what you've done!" cried the toys angrily. "You've torn off all the toy soldier's bearskin hat, and you've squashed his poor hand!"

The toy soldier was crying bitterly. Grumph was terribly upset – but it was done now! How he wished he had not been so unkind!

"What shall I do?" wailed the toy soldier. "Oh, what shall I do? When Billy and Betty see me, with my bearskin hat all torn off, and my hand squashed, they will throw me into the dustbin. Boo-hoo-hoo!"

"The rocking-horse had better take you to Santa Claus' workshop," said the teddy bear. "He knows the way because he came from there. He told me so. Perhaps Santa Claus can mend the toy soldier and make him better."

So the toys put the toy soldier on Grumph's back, and made him rock out of the nursery and down the garden towards the great hill where Santa Claus lived. It was miles away, and all through the night Grumph rocked hard, with the toy soldier on his back.

And at last he got there. Santa Claus heard the sound of his neighing and hrrumphing at the door and came to see who his visitor was.

Grumph explained, and the toy soldier showed his poor bearskin hat and squashed right hand. "Dear, dear!" said Santa Claus, looking severely at the rocking-horse. "I have heard of you and your stupid way of scaring the toys by rocking suddenly when they are near. Come in!"

The horse rocked in and Santa Claus took them to his workshop. He opened a drawer and looked into it.

"Dear me!" he said. "I've no bearskin left. It's all been used up. *Now* what am I to do?" He turned and looked at Grumph's mane. "You've a nice thick black mane!" he said, "I think you'll have to spare a little for the toy soldier!"

Then, to Grumph's horror, he took a pair of scissors and cut a big patch out of the horse's thick mane! How queer it looked!

Quickly and neatly, Santa Claus put the black hair on the toy soldier's head. He stuck it there with glue, and it soon dried. Then Santa looked at the toy soldier's squashed hand. He found a new hand and carefully put it on. It belonged to a doll, really, so it was pink, instead of black, and looked rather queer.

"Now I've no black paint!" said Santa in a vexed tone. "Only blue or red. Those won't do for a soldier's hand. Ha, Grumph! I'll have to take off one of your nice black spots, and use it for the soldier's hand. It will do nicely!"

He carefully scraped off a large spot on the horse's back, mixed it with a tiny drop of water and painted it on the toy soldier's new hand. It looked fine!

"Thank you very much indeed!" said the toy soldier, gratefully. "You are very kind."

"Not at all!" said Santa, beaming all over his big kind face. "I'm always ready to help toys, you know!"

Then off went Grumph home again, rocking hard all the way in order to get home by cockcrow. The toy soldier sat proudly on his back, glad of his new hat and new hand.

The toys cheered when they saw him. "What a glorious bearskin hat you have – and look at your fine new black hand!" they cried.

Grumph said nothing. He stood in the middle of the nursery floor, quite still, not a rock left in him.

"Santa took some of Grumph's hair for me, and one of Grumph's spots to paint my hand black," said the toy soldier. "You can see where he has a bare place on his mane, and one of his biggest spots is missing."

Sure enough, it was just as the toy soldier had said. The toys looked to see – and each of them thought that it served Grumph right.

And dear me, when Billy and Betty saw that Grumph had a bald place in his mane and one of his spots was missing, they *were* surprised. They couldn't think what had happened.

And now Grumph never scares the toys. He has certainly learnt his lesson!

Dame Thimble and her Matches

There was once an old woman called Dame Thimble who lighted her lamp as soon as it got dark each night. And every night she had to hunt for her matches. Sometimes they were on the mantelpiece, sometimes they were on the dresser, sometimes they were in the kitchen drawer and most often they were in the cupboard.

But, of course, it is hard to find matches when it is dark, and Dame Thimble bumped herself so often trying to find them that she decided to do something about it.

"I'll put them in my pocket in the morning," she said, "then when the evening comes I shall just have to put my hand in my pocket, and there I shall find the matches as easily as anything! I can light my lamp at once without hunting all over the place first!"

So in the morning she put the matches in her pocket, and then busied herself with her day's washing and ironing. She worked hard until tea-time, when she sat down and had a nice cup of tea. After tea she had to wash up and, as it was getting very dark by then, she wanted to light her lamp.

So she went to her cupboard to find her matches. They weren't there. Then she went to the kitchen dresser, but they weren't there either. Then she felt all along the mantelpiece and bumped her head on the corner of the bookcase nearby. But still she could find no matches.

"They must be in the kitchen drawer!" she said, and off she went to look there, treading on the cat on her way, poor thing, and bumping her knee against the stool.

There were no matches in the drawer, though Dame Thimble felt at the back as well as at the front.

"I'll go and ask Mister Todd if he'll lend me a box," she said at last. "I can't *think* where mine are!" So off she went next door to Mister Todd's. He opened the door to Dame Thimble, and when he heard that she wanted some matches he nodded his head.

"Yes, Dame Thimble, I will lend you some, but would you mind doing something for me in return? Would you go along the lane to the Bee-Woman's and ask her for a pot of honey? She said she would give me one to-day."

"Certainly," said Dame Thimble. So down the lane she went till she came to the Bee-Woman's hive-shaped cottage.

She knocked at the door and Bee-Woman opened it.

"Could you let me have the pot of honey you promised Mister Todd?" asked Dame Thimble.

"Oh Yes," said the Bee-Woman. "But I'll have to climb to my top shelf to get it. Would you go and ask Tompkins the cat who lives next door, to lend me his new ladder? Mine is broken."

"Very well," said the old dame, with a sigh, and off she went next door. Tompkins the cat opened the door to her and listened to what she wanted.

"Yes" he said. "I will lend the Bee-Woman my ladder, but I shall want something in return. Would you go down the lane and over the hill to where Diddle the Brownie lives and beg him to let me have a little of his fresh butter. I've quite run out of it to-day."

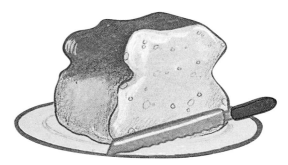

"I suppose I must, " said Dame Thimble, beginning to feel very tired. "I won't be long. Good-bye."

She walked all the way down the lane and over the hill to Diddle the Brownie's. She told him that Tompkins the cat had sent her to borrow a little fresh butter, and Diddle promised to get it from his dairy.

"Whilst I'm getting it, would you mind just popping next door to get a paper bag for it?" said Diddle. "I haven't one."

So Dame Thimble popped next door, and got a fine big paper bag from Tinkle the pixie, who, strangely enough, didn't want anything done in return!

Diddle put the butter into the paper bag and Dame Thimble took it, walked over the hill and up the lane, and at last came to the cottage of Tompkins the cat.

Then the old woman hurried to Mister Todd's cottage, and gave him the honey.

"Now, will you lend me some matches, Mister Todd?" she asked. "I really must have some to light my lamp."

He had fetched his ladder and gave it to Dame Thimble. She took it to the Bee-Woman, and helped her to raise it up to her top shelf. The Bee-Woman took down a small jar of honey from the shelf and handed it to Dame Thimble.

"Well, it's a funny thing now, but I can't seem to find my matches," said Mister Todd. They're in the bedroom somewhere. Let's go and look for them together, Dame Thimble. I'll take my kitchen candle with me."

So they went together into the bedroom, Mister Todd carrying his candle – but just as they entered the room the draught blew out the candle! And there they both were in the darkness.

"Well, *now* we're in a fix!" cried Mister Todd. "We shall go bumping into every-thing. Oh, dear, where can those matches be? We can't see to look for anything now. It's such a nuisance. We can't even light the candle till we've got some matches."

Now at that very moment Dame Thimble put her hand in her pocket, and what was her delight to feel a box of matches there! She took them out and struck one.

"Look, I've some matches in my pocket, Mister Todd! Now we can light the candle and hunt properly."

So they hunted with the lighted candle, but no matches could they find anywhere. Mister Todd got quite hot and bothered, and he took out his handkerchief to wipe his forehead – and out of his pocket fell – a box of matches!

"Oh, there they are!" he cried. "They were in my pocket all the time!"

"You stupid, silly creature!" cried Dame Thimble, quite losing her temper. "Here I've been going down on my hands and knees, poking in all the dusty corners of your bedroom and you had them in your pocket all the time! You are a big stupid, the biggest I've ever met. Fancy hunting all over the place for matches when they were in your pocket all the time! Why you didn't look there first I can't think! If I hadn't had *my* matches with me we couldn't even have lighted your candle!"

Mister Todd wiped his forehead and looked at Dame Thimble.

"Well," he said, "if you had your matches in your pocket all the time, why did you come here to borrow mine?"

Dame Thimble stared at Mister Todd. Dear me, what a very peculiar thing! Here she had been scolding him for doing exactly what she had done herself! She had popped her matches safely in her pocket so that she might find them easily, and then she had hunted all over her own cottage for them – which was just what Mister Todd had done. And she had called him stupid and silly, when she was just as bad herself!

"Oh my, oh my!" she groaned, sinking down into a chair, "I'm much sillier than you, Mister Todd. I've fetched honey from the Bee-Woman, a ladder from Tompkins the cat, a pat of butter from Diddle, and a paper bag from his next-door neighbour – and all because I didn't look in my pocket for my matches. I could cry, really I could!"

"No, don't do that," said Mister Todd, kindly. "Stay to supper with me instead, and we'll have hot cocoa and new bread and honey. You'd like that. We're two foolish people, so we ought to get on very well, and understand one another nicely."

So down they sat to hot cocoa and new bread and honey, and the very next week they got married – all because of a box of matches. Well, well, strange things do happen, don't they?

The Clever Toy Drum

Nobody in the toy cupboard liked the toy drum. For one thing it was rather big and took up a lot of room. And for another thing it made such a noise when the drum-sticks beat on the drum that all the dolls and animals were quite deafened.

"It's a noisy thing, that drum," said the toy soldier.

"It's too big for the toy cupboard," said the white teddy bear. "I shan't let it sleep here at night. I shall push it out on to the carpet!"

The white teddy bear was quite bold enough to do this, but the drum didn't wait to be pushed. Every night it quietly rolled itself out of the cupboard on to the carpet so as to give the toys more room, and stayed there all by itself. It was sad and lonely, for a drum likes jolly friends and chattering and noise – but it wouldn't push itself where it wasn't wanted.

"After all, I can't help being a drum," it thought puzzled. "I might have been a trumpet, or a toy soldier or even a white teddy bear. But I was made into a drum, and a drum must be round and it must make a noise."

Sometimes the drum tried to talk to Lucy Ann, the little golden-haired doll in the blue dress, who sat on a pretty chair just inside the toy cupboard. Lucy Ann didn't really mind the drum, but she pretended to be as grand as the others, and when the drum murmured a few words to her she turned her pretty back on it and wouldn't answer.

Then one night the toys decided to have a party. But they didn't ask the drum. Oh no! He was left out as usual. There were to be cakes, sandwiches and sweets, and afterwards the musical box had promised to play so the toys could dance. It would be a lovely party.

And then the toys discovered that they hadn't a doll's table big enough to put all the dishes on! So what do you think they did? Why, they pushed the drum into the middle of the nursery floor, whisked a white table-cloth over him, and used him for a table!

They never even asked him if they might. He would do for a table, so he must put up with it, they thought. They giggled when they thought of him, sitting quietly under the table-cloth, holding all the lovely things to eat. Silly old drum! Only Lucy Ann, the golden-haired doll, felt a little bit sorry for him. But she didn't like to say anything.

The drum was so surprised when it felt the cloth whisked over him and the dishes set down on him that he couldn't say a word. He was very angry indeed.

It was too bad of the toys! They hadn't even asked him to the party, that was the worst of it. If they had asked him, he would have been pleased to help them and be their table – but they were unkind and they treated him as if he hadn't any feelings at all.

The drum had half a mind to get up and roll away, cloth, dishes and all! That would upset the toys finely and spoil their party! All the cakes would go rolling on to the floor, all the sandwiches would be upset. The drum really thought he would do it.

Then he thought of Lucy Ann. Perhaps she would cry if he played such an unkind trick. She wasn't very nice to him, but she was so pretty and so sweet that

the drum was really very fond of her. So he stayed still and let the toys use him for their table.

Now just as they were in the middle of their party, the nursery door was pushed open, and in came Scamp, the puppy! He had smelt the cakes and sandwiches and had come to see where they were. When he saw the toys there, sitting round the drum-table, eating, he was surprised. He bounded up to them and tried to push them away with his nose.

The toys jumped up, screaming. They took up the dishes of cakes and the plates of sandwiches and ran into the toy

cupboard with them. They knew how greedy the puppy was. They didn't like him a bit.

Scamp was angry when he saw the toys taking away the cakes and sandwiches. He snatched the cloth off the drum to see if there were any cakes under it. Then he ran into the toy cupboard and sniffed about for the sandwiches he knew were hidden there. When he couldn't find them (because the clever toy soldier had hidden them in the brick box and shut down the lid), he was angrier than ever.

He took up the toy soldier and shook him hard. Then he took the white teddy bear and tore off his nice blue ribbon. After that he nibbled some hair off the biggest doll and bit the tail off the poor frightened plush monkey.

What a to-do there was! The toys were crying and shouting, nearly frightened to death. Lucy Ann crouched in a corner of the cupboard, hoping and hoping that the puppy wouldn't see her. But he did. He dragged her out by her pretty blue frock, and she bumped her head against the toy cupboard.

Now all this time the drum stood outside watching. You might have thought that he would have been glad to see the unkind toys punished like this by the puppy – but he wasn't. No, he was worried and frightened. He didn't like to hear the toy soldier crying and he couldn't bear to see the white teddy bear without his nice blue ribbon. It was dreadful. The toy drum felt very sorry for all the toys.

Ah, but when he heard pretty little Lucy Ann, the golden-haired doll, crying in fright when the puppy pulled her out of the toy cupboard, then something happened to the drum. He began to think harder than ever he had in his life before, because he couldn't bear to hear Lucy Ann crying like that.

"I must get help, somehow!" thought the drum, anxiously. "Oh, how can I get help? It's no use rolling out of the nursery to fetch the children, because they sleep in too high a bed for me to reach them. What can I do?"

Then he had a wonderful idea! He would beat himself with his two drum-sticks, and that would surely wake up the children! So up leapt the two drum-sticks and began to beat the drum as loudly as they could. Rub-a-dub-dub! Rub-a-dub-dub! RUB-A-DUB-DUB!

Now Molly and Tony, the two children, were fast asleep in bed when the drum began to beat, for it was night-time and everyone was sleeping. But when the sound of the toy drum came into their dreams they both woke up in a hurry! They knew the sound of the drum very well indeed, for they beat it every day when they played soldiers.

"Listen, Tony," said Molly. "That's our drum! What's it sounding for? Let's go and see!"

Out of bed they jumped and ran into the day nursery – and when they had put on the light they saw that rascal of a puppy shaking the toys like rats!

"Oh you wicked fellow!" said Tony, smacking the puppy hard. "You know you ought to stay in your basket down in the kitchen all night. Go back to it at once!"

The puppy ran away quickly. The children stood and looked at the drum. It had stopped beating itself as soon as it had heard them coming, and was now quite silent.

"Who beat the drum, I wonder?" said Molly, astonished. "One of the toys must have done it to waken us."

"Isn't that strange?" said Tony, sleepily. "I wonder which toy it was, Molly.

Well, we've rescued them from Scamp, so we might as well go back to bed now. I'm so sleepy."

They went back to bed and left the toys alone. At first they were too upset and too frightened to speak. Then they sat and thought to themselves – and they thought about the clever, kind little drum, that had saved them from that dreadful rough puppy. The drum might have left them all to be nibbled and shaken – but it hadn't. It had called for help. It was a good-hearted drum, and a smart one too.

The toy soldier got up first. He went to the drum. "Please forgive me for having been unkind to you," he said. "I'm sorry."

"So am I," cried the white teddy bear.

"And so are we!" cried all the rest.

Lucy Ann, the golden-haired doll, ran to the drum and flung her arms around him.

"You're a darling!" she said. "You're cleverer and kinder than all the rest of us together. You shall be my friend!"

Well, think of that! The drum trembled with delight and didn't know what to say. Then the toys fetched out their cakes and sandwiches and gave another party, this time for the little toy drum. And always after that they were kind to him and made him their friend.

But he still likes pretty little Lucy Ann the best of all.

He Didn't Believe in Fairies

There was once a farmer who didn't believe in fairies. You should have heard him laugh when fairies were mentioned! Why, he almost deafened you!

Now I expect you have heard it said that only those who believe in the Little Folk ever see them. Those who *don't* believe in them can't see them even when they are right under their noses!

And often the fairies play tricks on these people just to teach them.

Farmer Straw only believed in horses, cows, sheep and things like that. If you mentioned such things as dragons, unicorns, witches or pixies he would explode with laughter and call you a ninny. The fairy folk used to listen, and they laughed too. It really *was* funny to them, you see, to think that people said they weren't there, when *they* knew quite well they were!

Now Farmer Straw had a very fine mushroom field. So had his neighbour, Farmer Twinkle, and his other neighbour, Dame Busy. And in the autumn they all got up very early in the mornings and went mushrooming. When they sold their mushrooms in the market they made a great deal of money.

One night the little folk had had a dance in Dame Busy's field. It was a GRAND dance, with the grasshopper band playing rilloby-rill half the evening. That is the famous elfin tune, you know, that the grasshoppers know so well. There had been all kinds of games too, and a most delicious feast. And for once it hadn't ended at cockcrow, but just a little bit later.

Now this was a pity – because no sooner did the party break up than a rainstorm began! How it poured! How it pelted! The fairies, pixies and elves raced for the shelter of the mushrooms that had shot up in the night. They crouched beneath them and tried to keep their lovely frocks from being splashed. They hoped the rain would soon stop.

But it didn't. No, it went on and on and on. Goodness, the little folk couldn't possibly go home in it, they would be wet through! And see – there were lights in the farmhouses! People were getting up early to go mushrooming. Then what would happen to the fairies?

Dame Busy came out of her farmhouse with a big basket.

"Hey, little folk!" cried an elf. "We shall be caught here if Dame Busy arrives before we go. She believes in fairies, you know, so she'll see us here under the mushrooms. Let us quickly run to the mushrooms in the other field – those belonging to Farmer Twinkle."

So off the fairy folk scuttled through the wet grass and the rain, and soon they were safely sheltering under Farmer Twinkle's mushrooms. But dear me – it wasn't long before the farmer opened *his* farmhouse door and came out mushrooming too!

So off went the fairies again – this time to Farmer Straw's mushrooms. And bother me if *his* door didn't open and out he came, too, to go mushrooming!

"Our luck is out this morning!" cried an elf. "Whatever can we do? There are no more mushrooms to shelter us from this dreadful rainstorm! We shall have to go home and, oh dear, what colds we shall get, for we shall be soaked through!"

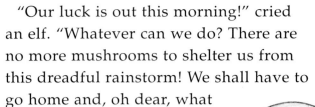

"No, don't let's get wet!" cried a pixie, "There's no need to! Let's each pick our mushroom and use it like the humans use umbrellas! We can carry them all the way home and never get wet at all! As for old Farmer Straw he won't see us for he doesn't believe in fairies! Ho ho!"

"Ho ho ho ho!" laughed all the little folk delightedly. Then they each picked a mushroom, and holding it above their bright little heads they made their way across the wet field down to the little wood where they lived.

Farmer Straw met them as he came to the field with his basket – yes, he met them – but he couldn't see the fairies, of course, because he didn't believe in them!

All he saw was a row of big mushrooms walking solemnly along in the rain! He stood and stared with his mouth wide open. Then he gave a scream of fright and ran back to his farm.

"Oh! Oh! I'm going mad! I've seen mushrooms walking! Oh, what shall I do?"

"Don't be so silly!" shouted Dame Busy and Farmer Twinkle. "It's only the little folk using them as umbrellas!"

"I don't believe in the fairies!" yelled Farmer Straw. "No, that I don't."

"Oh well, if you like to believe in mushrooms walking off by themselves, instead of in the little folk, you do as you like," said Dame Busy, scornfully. "But it seems to me to be much easier to believe in fairies than in walking mushrooms!"

Farmer Straw looked back at the row of bobbing mushrooms, half believing in the little folk for a moment – and just for that moment he saw a roguish face peeping at him from under a mushroom and caught a glint of a silver pair of wings. But it was gone in a flash.

"Only ninnies believe in fairies," he said. "I'm not a ninny. There's something gone wrong with my eyes this morning, that's all – or else I'm not properly awake yet. Ho – I'd rather believe in walking mushrooms than a dozen fairies! That I would!"

But I wouldn't. Would you? Anyway, Farmer Straw lost all his mushrooms that day and you should have heard the little folk laugh about it! Farmer Straw thought it was the swallows twittering – but it wasn't!

Sally Simple's Spectacles

Sally Simple had a fine pair of spectacles. They sat on her round nose beautifully, and looked very grand, for the glass was square, not round, and the frame was bright green. Sally Simple felt very fine indeed when she wore her spectacles. She didn't really need to wear any, for her eyes were perfectly good – but when she had seen those grand green spectacles in a shop, with their square glass, she had fallen in love with them and bought them!

One day Sally went to a sewing-meeting. She set off, in her best green blouse with yellow buttons, and her spectacles in a case. It was raining hard, so Sally put up her umbrella and went squelching through the mud.

There were a lot of people at the sewing-meeting. Old Dame Twinkle was there, and Mother Hubbard. Mrs. Pippitty was there and Mrs. Popoff. The meeting was quite crowded. Sally Simple was pleased.

"There will be all the more people to see my beautiful glasses," she thought to herself. She sat down at a table, and put her umbrella beside her, for she was always afraid that some one else might take it if she put it into the umbrella stand.

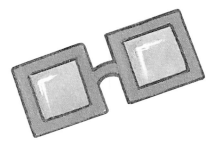

Sally took out her spectacle case and opened it. She put her marvellous green spectacles on her round nose and looked to see if anyone was admiring them.

"Goodness, Sally!" said Dame Twinkle, her shining face all over smiles. "What do you want spectacles for? Your eyes are as good as mine any day!"

"And what queer ones they are!" said Mother Hubbard.

"They cost a lot of money," said Sally Simple offended. "They are the very latest fashion. Your bonnet, Mother Hubbard, is much queerer than my spectacles. It must be more than fifty years old."

"Now, now!" said Mrs. Popoff. "No quarrelling, please. I am sure, Sally, that your spectacles will help you sew beautifully!"

Sally put her glasses firmly on her nose and bent over her work. "Everyone is jealous of me because I have such fine spectacles," she thought. "Well, let them be!"

Now Sally soon found that she could see better without the new spectacles than with. They were not made for *her* eyes, and they hurt them. What a nuisance! Sally began to blink and wink – but she did not want to take them off – no! What would be the good of buying them if she didn't wear them?

But when tea-time came Sally Simple took them off and put them on the table. She did like to see properly all that she was eating. She ate tomato sandwiches and cucumber sandwiches. She ate brown bread and butter and strawberry jam. She ate a ginger bun, a chocolate cake, and two slices of cherry cake – and she drank four cups of tea. So she enjoyed herself very much, and laughed and joked with the rest.

But when tea was over, Sally thought she would put her beautiful glasses on again, and she looked for them – but, dear me, they were gone!

"I put them on the table, just here!" said Sally Simple, and she looked everywhere on the table for her lovely glasses. But they weren't there! She looked in the cotton box. She looked among the scissors. She unrolled the roll of cloth nearby. But nowhere could she see her precious glasses!

"Has somebody taken my glasses?" asked Sally in a loud voice. "They are gone! I simply must have them to wear whilst I am sewing."

"*I* haven't seen them," said Mother Hubbard.

"Nor have I," said Dame Twinkle.

"I expect Sally's got them herself," said Mrs. Pippitty. "Have you looked in your pocket, Sally?"

"Of course, I have," said Sally. "I've looked everywhere!"

"They may be on the floor," said Mrs. Popoff. So everyone put down scissors, sewing, and needles, and hunted on the floor for Sally's' spectacles. But they were nowhere to be seen. It was really most mysterious. The empty case was in Sally's pocket – but the glasses seemed to have disappeared completely.

"There is only one thing I can think," said Sally, pursing her lips.

"And what is that?" asked Dame Twinkle.

"Well – I think *one* of you has taken my new spectacles," said Sally. "I know some people felt jealous of them! Now, who is it? I tell you, I really must have them back because they cost a lot of money."

"Sally! You should not say that one of us has taken your silly glasses," said Mother Hubbard crossly. "They are *not* silly," said Sally.

"They are – *very*!" said Mother Hubbard.

"They are *not*!" said Sally, going red.

"Now, now!" said Mrs. Popoff. "I expect they will turn up soon. Shall we all open our work-bags and see if the glasses have got there by mistake?"

So everyone opened her basket and tipped out cottons and silks and needles – but nobody had those glasses, it seemed. It was most peculiar. "Well, I simply don't know where they can have gone to, Sally," said Mrs. Pippitty. "Let us get on with our work again now. We have wasted quite enough time."

right up to her neck. She set her hat straight. She put on her gloves and buttoned them. Then she took her umbrella and walked to the door.

"Sally, don't go in a temper like this," said Mrs. Popoff kindly. "It is foolish of you. Your glasses will turn up somewhere, and then you will be sorry,"

"I shall *not* be sorry!" said Sally, who was most upset. She opened the door. It was pouring with rain. Dear, dear, what wet weather!

"And I hope that whoever has my glasses will be WELL PUNISHED!" said Sally. She opened her umbrella – and oh, my goodness me, out of it fell something that shone and glittered – something that fell to the ground – and smashed into a hundred shining little pieces – Sally's beautiful green glasses!

They had slipped off the table into her umbrella, as it stood by her knee at tea-time. No-one had thought of looking in Sally's own umbrella! Everyone stared and stared.

"Well, Sally," said Mother Hubbard, at last, "your wish has come true. You said that you hoped that whoever had your glasses would be well punished – and you were the one that had them – and you have been punished because they have broken."

"Well, I shall not stay here a minute more," said Sally Simple in a rage. "*Someone* has my glasses – my beautiful green glasses – and I shall go home and not come to this horrid, nasty sewing-meeting any more!"

"Don't be silly, Sally," said Mother Hubbard. But Sally's mind was made up. She was not going to stay and sew without her glasses! She got up from her seat and took down her mackintosh from its peg. She put it on, and buttoned it

Poor Sally Simple! She did feel so ashamed of herself – and there were her lovely glasses, smashed to bits – all because she had walked out in a temper! Tears poured down Sally's cheeks. Kind Mrs. Popoff saw them and came running to Sally. She put her arm around her.

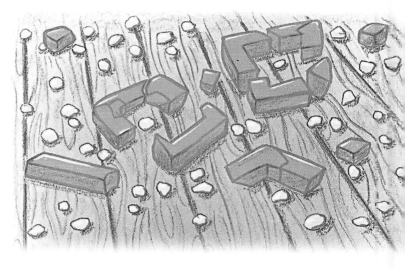

"Never mind," she said. "You look *so* much nicer without spectacles, Sally, dear. And besides, I am sure they were bad for your eyes, because they made you wink and blink. So don't worry any more. Come and take your things off again, and do a bit more sewing."

Sally was so ashamed of herself that all she wanted to do was to go home – but Mrs. Popoff was so kind that she went back again into the room and took off her things.

"I beg everybody's pardon," she said in a little voice. "It was very foolish and wrong of me."

And after that Sally Simple didn't buy any more spectacles – because her eyes really were very good indeed. She is much nicer now, so perhaps it was a good thing those green glasses were smashed to bits. What do *you* think?

The Beautiful Cricket Ball

The boys were going to play cricket. There were the twins, Peter and John, Alec, Tom, Jim, Fred, Ian, and Hugh. What fun it would be!

"We will play on that nice smooth stretch of sand!" said Peter. "You put the stumps in, John!"

Little Harry came running up. "Peter, Peter!" he cried. "Can I play too?"

"No," said Peter. "You're too small."

"But I can run fast," said Harry. "Oh, do let me play, Peter. I won't ask to bat – just let me field for you."

"No, we've got enough players," said Peter. "Run along and play with your sister, Harry."

Harry was very disappointed. He had so hoped to play cricket with the big boys. It would have been such fun. He could run very fast and, although he didn't bat very well, he could bowl quite straight.

He went off, hurt and sad. Peter might have given him a chance!

His little sister was building a castle. "Come and help, Harry," she said. Harry took up his spade and began to dig. It was no good being horrid to Susan just because someone had been horrid to *him*!

The boys drove in the stumps – and then Fred brought out a most beautiful new cricket ball.

"Look, boys," he said. "Here's a fine ball! I had it for my birthday yesterday!"

"My!" said Peter and the others, looking at the beautiful ball admiringly. "That's a beauty! Can we play with it to-day, Fred?"

"Yes," said Fred, proudly. "But will you let me bat first if I let you play with my new ball?"

"All right," said the others. "Take the bat, Fred. Who's going to bowl? You, John! See if you can get Fred out with his own ball?"

The game began. Harry, still digging castles, could hear the click of the ball against the bat as Fred drove it over the sand and then ran. The boys shouted. They ran after the ball and threw it in. John stopped bowling and Ian began. It all looked very jolly indeed, and Harry wished and wished he could have played too.

At last Fred was bowled out. He gave up the bat to Peter, who was a very good batsman indeed. Hugh took the fine new ball to bowl to Peter. It felt so good as he twirled it about – the best ball the boys had ever had to play with!

Hugh bowled, and Peter struck out. The ball flew along the sand, and Peter ran, and ran and ran. He meant to make more runs than anyone else that morning! At last the ball was thrown in again and Hugh caught it. He bowled it to Peter again. Peter slashed out with the bat. Click! Went the ball. The ball flew towards the rocks.

"Stop it, Ian, stop it!" yelled Fred. "Don't let it go among the rocks, or we shall lose it."

But Ian could not stop it, for the ball was going too fast. It rolled fast towards the rocks. It struck once and flew up into the air – then it dropped somewhere.

"Find it, find it, Ian!" yelled everyone.

"Hurry! Peter is making more runs than anyone!"

Ian hunted round the rocks. He could not see the ball anywhere. How he hunted! He looked under the seaweed. He looked in every pool. That beautiful new ball was not to be seen!

At last the others came to help him look too. They peered here and there, they splashed into the pools, but it wasn't a bit of good – that ball could *not* be found!

"It's gone," said Fred, very much upset. "Quite disappeared. What shall we do?"

"Better play with our old one," said John. So the old one was got out and the game went on. But everyone was very sad about Fred's fine new ball. It was too bad to lose it the very first game.

Harry had been digging all the time the boys were hunting for the ball. He didn't like to go near them, for he was afraid they would send him away again. He did not know whether they had found the ball or not – but when he saw them playing again he thought they must have found their ball. He didn't know it was the old one.

The castle was finished at last. Susan wanted to do something else. "Let's go shrimping," she said.

"All right," said Harry. "We'll catch some shrimps for your tea, Susan."

They took their shrimping nets and went to the rockpools. They pushed their nets through the sand and looked to see how many shrimps they had caught.

"Only one tiny crab," said Susan, and she and Harry put their nets in the water again.

"I can see a big prawn!" suddenly shouted Harry, in delight. "Hurrah! Come here into my net, prawn!" But the prawn would not be caught. He darted here and there, and at last disappeared under a shelving rock that jutted out into the pool. Harry stuck his net under the rock to catch the prawn.

He drew his net out and looked into it – no – there was no prawn there!

"Harry, something rolled out from under that rock when you stuck your net there," said Susan, pointing. "What was it?"

Harry looked down into the pool. He saw a big red ball there. He picked it up. "It must have been under that ledge of rock," he said. "And when I poked my net underneath it must have made the ball roll out. I wonder whose ball it is."

"It belongs to those boys," said Susan. "I heard them say they hadn't found their ball. They are playing with another one."

"Are they really, Susan?" said Harry. "This must be Fred's beautiful new ball then. He must have been upset when it couldn't be found."

"Are you going to take it back to them?" asked Susan.

"I don't know, " said Harry. "They were horrid to me this morning. I don't see why I should be nice to them."

"But Fred will be so sad if he doesn't get his new ball back," said kind-hearted Susan. "Don't you remember how bad we felt when we lost our new kite, Harry?"

"Yes," said Harry. "All right, I'll take it back to the boys."

He dried the ball on a towel, and then ran to where the boys were playing. He waited until the batsman was bowled out and then yelled to Peter:

"Peter! I've found Fred's new ball! It was in the rock-pool, catch!"

The boys turned in surprise. Fred gave a cheer. "Hurrah! I'm so glad!"

Peter caught the ball and stared at Harry. "That's jolly good of you," he said. "You are a sport! I say, boys, what about letting him come into the game? He must be a good sort to bring back our ball when we wouldn't let him play this morning!"

"Yes, let him come!" roared all the boys. "Come on, young

Harry! We'll let you play with us. It was decent of you to give back our ball!"

So Harry joined the game – and wasn't he pleased and proud. He fields very well indeed and, do you know, although he only made one run, he bowled out Ian and Hugh. The boys were quite surprised.

"You play a good game, Harry," said Peter, at the end. "You can come and play with us again to-morrow."

Now Harry always plays cricket with the big boys – and how glad he is that he took Susan's advice and was nice to the boys when he really didn't want to be! As for Fred's beautiful new ball, they are still playing with it. Its stay in the rock-pool didn't hurt it a bit!

Chapter 2

The Birds and the Bun

There was once a baker's boy who went down Leafy Lane with a basket of bread and buns. As he went he sang a song and swung his basket, and out dropped a bag with a large currant bun inside. The boy did not see the bun falling and he went on his way. The bun lay in the lane in its paper bag, and as no one came by that way it stayed there for a whole hour.

Then a robin came by and saw it. "A paper bag, a paper bag!" he cried.

A brown sparrow flew down and pecked at the bag. "There's something inside!" he chirrupped.

Down flew a fine chaffinch and pecked open the bag. "I have pecked a hole!" he sang, "I have pecked a hole!"

Then a big blackbird fluttered down and put his head inside the hole. "There is a bun inside!" he sang. "A bun, a big currant bun!"

A thrush joined the little crowd and he pecked at the bun. "It is good!" he said. "I shall eat it. It is mine."

"Yours!" cried the robin, indignantly. "What do you mean? I saw the paper bag first!"

"But I told you there was something inside the bag!" chirrupped the sparrow, at once. "I did, I did!"

The chaffinch pushed against the thrush. "Go away!" He cried. "This is my bun. It was I who pecked a hole in the bag."

"But I peeped inside it!" said the blackbird. "The bun is mine. Go away, everybody!"

"You are foolish!" said the thrush, scornfully. "I pecked the bun first – so it is mine. I am now going to eat it!"

Then there was such a noise of quarrelling and chirrupping and singing that no one could hear himself speak. Suddenly there was a large caw and down flew a large black rook.

"What is the matter?" he said, in his deep voice.

Then everyone told him about the bun in the paper bag.

"And each of us thinks it is his," said the thrush. "How can we settle it?"

"I will settle it for you," said the rook. "Now, you all have good voices, I will hear you sing for this bun, and I will give it to the one who sings the best."

"That is a good idea," cried everyone, for they all thought they had fine voices, even the shrill sparrows.

"Very well," said the rook. "Now please turn round so that you have your backs to me. When I say 'Go!' open your beaks and sing loudly for all you are worth, till I say stop."

So the robin, the sparrow, the chaffinch, the thrush and the blackbird all turned round with their backs to the rook, opened their beaks, and waited for him to say "Go!"

"Go!" he shouted. And then you should have heard the robin's creamy trill, the sparrow's loud chirrup, the chaffinch's pretty rattle of a song, the thrush's lovely notes and the blackbird's fluting. Really, it was fine to hear. They went on and on and on – and they didn't hear the rook tearing open the paper bag. They didn't hear him taking out the bun. They didn't hear him spreading his great black wings and flying off into the next field. No, they went on and on singing, each trying to outsing the rest.

When they were quite tired of singing, they wondered why the rook did not tell them to stop. So the robin looked round – and he saw that the rook was gone!

He hopped over to the paper bag – and it was empty!

"See, see!" he cried. "The bun is gone – and so is the rook! He has tricked us! Oh, the rascal! Oh, the scamp! Now we have lost our bun!"

"And there was plenty there for all of us!" chirrupped the sparrow, in dismay. "Why did we make such a fuss? We could each have had some – and now we have none!"

They flew off in a rage – and you may be sure the rook didn't show himself for a day or two! And when he did, and happened to meet the others, he cawed politely, and said: "Really, my friends, you have REMARKABLY fine singing voices! Do let me hear you some other time!"

And you should hear them shout at him then!

A Basket of Surprises

When Jimmy's mother went to the Garden Fair at the Vicarage she brought a very beautiful basket. It was large and round and deep, and had a fine, strong handle. All round the basket was a pretty green and yellow pattern. It really was a very fine basket, and Jimmy's mother was pleased with it.

"Now, you are not to borrow this basket for anything, Jimmy," she said to him. "You can have my old one if you want one. This is to be kept for special things, like taking eggs to Granny, or something like that."

Jimmy promised. He was once allowed to take some flowers in the basket to old Mr. White, but that was all. And then one day he wanted a basket to take his trains, signals and lines to his friend's, Billy Brown. He went to find the old basket and it wasn't there. His mother was out and no one was at home except Tibby, the big tabby cat, sitting by the fire.

"Where's the old basket, Tibby?" Jimmy asked her, but she just mewed and sat on by the fire, thinking her pussy thoughts. Jimmy hunted everywhere. There was no old basket to be found at all. Perhaps his mother had taken it.

"Well, I'll have to take the new basket," said Jimmy. "I can't possibly take all my things without a basket."

So he took down the beautiful new basket and packed his things into it.

Then off he went to Billy's and had a fine tea and a fine game. Billy begged him to lend him his railway for a day, so Jimmy said he would. He set off home with the empty basket, swinging it by the big handle.

He had to go through the woods on his way home, and as he ran he saw a bird fly into a bush. "Hello!" thought Jimmy. "There's a nest there. I'll just peep and see. I won't disturb the bird in case it deserts its nest – but I would just like to see if there are any baby birds there."

He pushed his way into the bush, but the bird flew out again and into another bush. Jimmy followed her. He felt sure she must have a nest somewhere. But she hadn't. She was just looking for the caterpillars there.

Jimmy set off home again – but suddenly he remembered that he had put down his basket somewhere. Goodness! Where could it be?

He ran back – but no matter how he looked he couldn't find that basket anywhere! "Oh, dear!" thought Jimmy, as he hunted. "Whatever will Mummy say if I go home without it? I am sure I put it down by the bush I first looked in."

But Jimmy couldn't find the bush! And at last he had to go home without the basket. When he told his mother he had lost it she was very cross.

"You are a naughty boy, Jimmy," she said. "I told you not to borrow my best basket. Now, unless it is found again, you must save up your money and buy me a new one."

"Oh, but Mummy, I'm saving up to buy a railway tunnel!" cried Jimmy, in dismay.

"Well, I'm sorry, dear, but you can't buy your tunnel until you have bought a new basket," said his mother. "You had better go and have another hunt for it."

Poor Jimmy! He went and hunted and hunted, but he could not find that basket! The next day his Uncle Peter came to see him and gave him some money to spend – but his mother said to put it all in his money-box to save up for the new basket. He was dreadfully disappointed. The next morning his mother called him and said: "Have you seen Tibby, Jimmy? She isn't in her usual place by the fire, and she hasn't been in for her breakfast."

"No, I haven't seen her," said Jimmy quite worried, for he was very fond of Tibby. "Where can she be?"

"Perhaps she will come in for her dinner," said his mother. But Tibby didn't. There was no sign of her at all. Jimmy got more and more worried. He had had Tibby from a kitten, and the two were great friends. He did so hope she hadn't got caught in a trap.

"Do you think she has, Mummy?" he asked. "Oh, wouldn't it be dreadful if she had gone rabbiting in the woods and got caught in a trap and nobody was there to set her free?"

"Oh, I don't expect she has, for a moment," said his mother. "She hardly ever goes rabbiting. She will turn up, I expect. Now, what are you going to do this afternoon, Jimmy? You said you wanted to go and play with Billy Brown."

"Well, I did want to," said Jimmy. "But I think I'll just go and hunt for Tibby, Mummy, I do feel unhappy about her, really I do."

"After tea we will catch the bus and go into the town to buy a new basket," said his mother. "I really must have another. I think you have enough money in your box to buy me one."

Jimmy went off to hunt for Tibby, feeling very miserable. "I've lost Tibby, and I've got to give up my railway tunnel and buy a new basket instead," he sighed, as he ran along to the woods. "What a lot of bad luck all at once!"

He soon came to the woods, and he began hunting about, calling Tibby. He felt sure she must have been caught in a trap.

"Tibby, Tibby, Tibby!" he cried. "Where are you? Tibby, Tibby, Tibby!"

For some time he could hear nothing but the wind in the trees and the singing of the birds. Then he thought he heard a small mew.

"Tibby!" he shouted. "Tibby!"

"Miaow!" said a pussy-voice, and up ran Tibby to Jimmy, and purred and rubbed herself against his legs.

"Oh, dear Tibby!" said Jimmy, really delighted to see his cat again. He picked her up in his arms and made a fuss of her. She purred loudly, and then tried to get down.

"No, I'll carry you home, Tibby," said Jimmy, and he turned to go home.
But Tibby struggled very hard,

and at last he had to let her go. She ran into the woods and disappeared. Jimmy was very much puzzled. He went after her.

"Tibby! Why don't you want to come home with me?" he called. "Come back! Where are you going?"

Tibby mewed from somewhere; then Jimmy saw her bright green eyes looking at him from a nearby bush! He ran up and knelt down to see where she was.

And, will you believe it, Tibby was lying comfortably down in the fine new basket that Jimmy had lost when he was looking for the bird's nest! There she was, as cosy as anything, looking up at Jimmy.

But there was still another surprise for the little boy for, when Tibby jumped out of the basket, what do you suppose he saw at the bottom? Why, five beautiful little Tabby kittens, all exactly like Tibby! He stared and stared and stared! He simply couldn't believe his eyes!

"Oh Tibby!" he said. "Oh Tibby! I've found you – and the basket – and some kittens too! Oh, whatever will Mummy say!"

He picked up the basket with the kittens and set off home. Tibby ran beside him mewing. When he got home he called his mother and showed her his surprising find.

She was just as astonished as he was! "Oh, Tibby, what darling little kittens!" she cried. "You shall have them in your own cosy basket by the fire! Fancy you finding our basket in the woods and putting your kittens there!"

"Mummy, I needn't spend my money on a new basket now, need I?" said Jimmy, pleased. "I can buy my tunnel with my money."

"Of course!" said his mother. "We will just put Tibby comfortably in her own basket with the kittens, and then we will catch the bus and go and buy your tunnel. You deserve it, really, Jimmy, because you gave up your afternoon's play with Billy to go and hunt for Tibby – and you found a basket of surprises, didn't you?"

So everyone was happy, and Jimmy got his railway tunnel after all. As for Tibby, she was very happy to be made such a fuss of, and you should have seen her kittens when they grew! They were the prettiest, dearest little things you could wish to see. I know, because, you see, I've got one of them for my own!

Tit for Tat

Jennifer, the curly-haired doll, had a little hairbrush of her own. She was very proud of it indeed, and the toys liked it, too, because it was fun to brush out Jennifer's lovely golden curls at night. Sometimes she lent it to the toys. Then the teddy bear brushed his short fur, the toy soldier brushed his bearskin hat, the pink cat brushed his coat and the clockwork mouse brushed his whiskers.

The little hairbrush lived in a small box with a little comb. Nobody used the comb because it was very small and it really wasn't any use for combing out Jennifer's thick curls. Sally, the little girl who owned all the toys, never bothered about the hairbrush at all. She hadn't brushed Jennifer's hair once with it, so it was a good thing the toys took turns at brushing it to make it look nice.

Then one day a most annoying thing happened. Sally was turning out her dolls' house and she wanted a brush to sweep the little carpets. She didn't want to borrow Mummy's brush because it was much too big for the tiny carpets.

So you can guess what she did. She borrowed Jennifer's little hairbrush. Just the thing!

"It's fine," said Sally, brushing away at the carpet. "Just right for this job. What a good thing I thought of it."

But the toys didn't think so at all! They looked on in dismay and Jennifer was almost in tears. Her own little hairbrush. How *mean* of Sally!

"Now I shan't be able to brush my hair with it any more," she thought. "It will be dirty and dusty and horrid. Oh, I do think Sally might have used something else. It's too bad of her."

Sally finished brushing the carpets and looked at the little brush. Such hard sweeping had almost worn it out.

"It's no use now," she said. "I'll throw it away." And into the fire it went! Oh, dear! The toys watched it blaze into flames for a minute or two – and then it was gone!

Jennifer, the curly-haired doll, cried that night. "I did like my little hairbrush," she said. "I've got such a lot of hair that I need a brush for it. Sally never brushes it for me. She doesn't look as if she brushes her own hair, either."

"She's an untidy little girl," said the bear. "She doesn't brush her teeth either. But she tells her mother that she does. She's a naughty story-teller."

"So she is," said the pink cat. "Do you know, her mother gave her a beautiful new green toothbrush last week and Sally hasn't used it yet? She hasn't cleaned her teeth all week."

"Then a toothbrush is just *wasted* on her!" said the clockwork mouse. "It's a pity we can't take it and use it to brush Jennifer's hair each night!"

"Dear me," said the bear, "that's a very fine idea, Mouse! Really very clever indeed. However did you think of it?"

The clockwork mouse would have blushed with delight at this praise if he could. "I don't know how I thought of it," he said. "I must be cleverer than I imagined."

"Shall we get Sally's toothbrush then?" said the pink cat. "I could climb up to the basin in the bathroom and reach up for it, I think. It's in her mug."

"All right. You go then," said the bear, and the pink cat went. He was quite good at jumping. He leapt up to the basin, slithered down into it, climbed up on to the shelf above, took Sally's perfectly new toothbrush in his mouth and jumped down to the floor again.

He padded into the playroom with it. The toys looked at it.

"The handle's too long," said the bear. "Much too long."

"Cut a bit off then," said the pink cat.

"What with?" asked the mouse.

"Sally's got some tools in a box," said Jennifer, the doll. "There's a little saw there. Couldn't we use that?"

Well, they could, of course, and they did! They found the little saw, and the bear sawed away valiantly at the handle of the toothbrush. Everyone watched in excitement.

The end of the handle suddenly fell off. The mouse picked up the little brush in delight. "Its handle is nice and short now," he said. "Just right for a hairbrush. Jennifer, do let me brush your hair for you."

So he was the first to brush the doll's curly hair with the new brush. It brushed beautifully because the bristles were harder than the ones in the hairbrush. Jennifer was delighted.

"Where shall we keep this brush?" asked the bear. "Better not put it into the box because Sally might see it."

"Put it into me," said the little tin teapot, in a spouty voice. "Sally never plays with me now. She'll never look inside me."

So that is where the toys keep the new hairbrush, in case you want to know.

The bear was a little bit worried at first. "Do you think we've done wrong to use Sally's toothbrush?" he said.

"Well, Sally took *my* brush and now we've taken hers, so it's tit for tat," said the curly-haired doll. "Anyway, she never used her toothbrush! We wouldn't have taken it if she did."

I'm just wondering what is going to happen when Sally's mother discovers that Sally's toothbrush is gone. It's going to be *very* difficult for naughty little Sally to make her mother believe that she is cleaning her teeth each night with a toothbrush that isn't there!

Holes in his Stockings

Mister Ho-Hhum was a brownie with twinkling eyes and a merry smile. He worked hard and was generous and good tempered – but there was just on thing he was always forgetting to do; and that was to mend the holes in his stockings.

His friend, Mister Hum-Hho, used to scold Ho-Hhum loudly, when he saw him taking off his shoes in the evening, and spied the enormous holes in the toes and heels of his stockings.

"Ho-Hhum!" he would cry. "Look at that dreadful hole, with your toe poking out! I'm ashamed of you. Why, don't you mend your stockings?"

"It doesn't matter," Ho-Hhum would say, with a grin. "Nobody sees them when I walk out. I don't take off my shoes in the street."

"Well, one day you *might* have to!" said Hum-Hho, "And then think how dreadful you would feel when everyone saw your toes poking through your stockings. I hope I'm not with you when *that* happens!"

"You needn't worry," said Ho-Hhum, gaily. "I shall NEVER take off my shoes in the street, so nobody will EVER see the holes in my stockings!"

And the naughty brownie went on wearing holey stockings every day – till something happened.

One Saturday morning he and Hum-Hho went out for a walk together, for it was a very fine day. They went round by the King's palace, and as they walked they heard the little Prince Peronel playing and shouting in the garden. Then suddenly they heard him cry bitterly.

The two brownies pushed open the garden door and rushed into the palace garden. They saw that the little Prince had tumbled out of his toy motor-car and had bumped his head One wheel was off the car and lay nearby on the ground.

Ho-Hhum picked up the little boy and wiped his tears. Hum-Hho picked up the motor car. Prince Peronel wept to see the wheel off.

"Now what shall I do?" he cried. "I can't ride in it!"

"If you've a hammer I could put the wheel on for you," said Ho-Hhum, kindly.

"I'm not allowed to have a hammer," said the little Prince. "But I know what you could do, brownie. Couldn't you take off your big, strong shoe and use that to knock my wheel on with? Oh, couldn't you?"

Mister Ho-Hhum thought he could quite well – and then, oh, my goodness me, he remembered that he had a great big hole in each of his stockings, and the holes would show dreadfully if he took his shoes off. Then what would the Prince think? He might even tell the King and Queen about the brownie that had holes in his stockings. So he shook his head.

"No," he said. "I can't use one of my shoes. I'll use a stone instead."

So he picked up a stone and tried to knock the wheel on with that. But the stone broke to pieces and a little bit flew off and cut the Prince's hand. He began to cry again and the two brownies were terribly upset.

"Why didn't you use your shoe as the Prince asked you?" said Hum-Hho to Ho-Hhum, quite forgetting that his friend had dreadful holes in his stockings. "Don't cry, little Prince. I'll knock the wheel on with one of *my* shoes!"

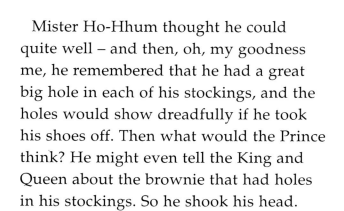

So Hum-Hho quickly slipped off one of his shoes and in a trice he had knocked the wheel on to the toy motor-car and mended it! Peronel was delighted.
He jumped in and rode down the path, calling loudly:

"Nurse! Mother! A kind brownie has mended my motor for me! Can he come to tea?"

Then, to the brownies' great surprise, who should come running down the path but the Fairy Queen herself, all in silver, shining like the moon. She kissed the little Prince and listened to what he had to say.

"I want this brownie to come to tea with me," he said, taking hold of Hum-Hho's hand. "Not the other one. He's unkind. He wouldn't take his shoe off and mend my wheel for me. But this one did."

Poor Ho-Hhum! He turned very red and ran out of the garden as fast as he could. As for Hum-Hho, he was so pleased at being asked for tea at the palace that he could hardly say a word! Off he went with the little Prince and had a lovely time. When he got home again, he called at Ho-Hhum's house to tell him about it.

And what was Ho-Hhum doing? Do you know? Of course you do! He was sitting on a stool, and round him were nine pairs of stockings, all with holes in – and Ho-Hhum was mending them as fast as he could.

"Don't scold me, Hum-Hho!" he cried, when he saw his friend. "I couldn't take my shoe off to mend the wheel because of the dreadful holes in my stocking. And now I am never going to have holey stockings again! Oh, how ashamed I felt to think I couldn't help the Prince!"

And two big tears rolled on to his darning-needle. Poor Ho-Hhum! Never mind, he has never had a hole in his stockings since that day!

The Sneezing Donkey

Once upon a time there was a small grey donkey who lived in a farm field and ate the grass and the thistles there. As he wandered across the field he felt a tickling in his nose. He lifted up his head and sneezed.

"A-tish-ee-aw!" he sneezed. "A-tish-ee-aw!"

His nose tickled again. He sneezed even more loudly. "A-TISH-ee-aw!"

He blinked and looked around. He could quite well feel another sneeze coming.

It came. "A-TISH-EE-TISH-EE-TISH-EE-AW!" he went, so loudly that some geese nearby fled away in alarm.

The donkey looked around, and to his surprise it had begun to pour with rain.

"That was my big sneeze did that," he thought to himself, pleased. "I have made it rain. I am really very clever. I shall tell everyone what I have done."

So he cantered over to the sheep and spoke to them. "Sheep, listen to me. Do you see this pouring rain? Well, I made it come when I sneezed so loudly!"

"How clever you are!" said the sheep admiringly. "Nothing happens when *we* sneeze!"

The donkey ran to the old brown horse and spoke to him, too. "Horse, listen to me. Do you see this pouring rain? Well, I made it come when I sneezed so loudly!"

"How clever you are!" said the horse admiringly. "Nothing happens when *I* sneeze!"

The donkey did feel proud. He wondered who else he could tell. He saw the hens and the cock at the end of the field and he trotted over to them. They were sheltering under the big hedge.

"Hens and cock, listen to me. Do you see this pouring rain? Well, I made it come when I sneezed so loudly!"

"How clever you are!" said the hens and cock admiringly. "Nothing happens when *we* sneeze – but thewn, we never *do* sneeze."

The donkey swung his long tail about, and wondered if he could tell anyone else. He saw the farm dog lying down in his tub and he cantered over to him.

"Rover, listen to me. Do you see this pouring rain? Well, I made it come by sneezing so loudly."

"How clever of you!" said Rover admiringly. "Nothing happens when *I* sneeze!"

The ducks came waddling by in a row, going to the pond. They were delighted with the rain. The donkey ran over to them.

"Ducks, listen to me," he said. "Do you see

this pouring rain? Well, *I* made it come when I sneezed so loudly."

"How clever of you!" said the ducks admiringly. "Nothing happens when *we* sneeze – but how we'd like it to rain whenever we sneeze!"

The donkey was so pleased with himself that he simply didn't know what to do.

The rain went on falling. It rained all day. It rained all night. It went on raining the next day too.

The sheep got tired of the rain. The brown horse got tired of the rain. The hens and the cock got tired of the rain. Rover got tired of the

rain. Everywhere was muddy. Everyone was wet and cold. Only the ducks liked the rain.

The sheep, the horse, the hens, cock and dog gathered together by the hedge and grumbled to one another.

"Look what that silly donkey has done with his sneezing! No one would have minded just a shower – but why should he make it rain all day and night like this? Let's go and tell him to stop the rain now."

So they went to the donkey. He was standing under a tree thinking how marvellous it was to have sneezed so much rain down.

"Donkey, we are wet and cold. Stop this rain at once," neighed the horse. "Donkey, our feathers are dripping. Stop this rain," clucked the hens and cock.

"Donkey, I have a feeling I shall bite your long tail if you don't sneeze again and *stop* the rain!" barked Rover, who could be very fierce.

The donkey stared at everyone in alarm. It had been easy enough to begin the rain – but he wasn't at all sure he could stop it. Besides, he couldn't sneeze unless a sneeze came. Whatever was he to do?

"The ducks like the rain," he said at last.

"If I stop the rain they will be angry and come and peck me."

"Well, we will be angrier and we will bite you, and nibble you and peck you too!" cried all the animals and birds at once.

"I don't know how to sneeze unless a sneeze happens to come," said the donkey, "and I don't know how to stop the rain."

"Well, why do you start a thing you don't know how to stop?" wuffed Rover crossly. "I shall snap at each of your legs!"

"And I shall butt you with my head," said the sheep.

"And I shall kick you with my heels," said the horse.

"And we will peck you with our beaks," said the birds. So they all began. They were so busy teasing the poor donkey that no one noticed that the clouds were blowing away – and the rain was stopping – and the sun was shining! But that was what was happening. The fields shone and glittered in the sun – it was a really lovely day.

"Stop! Stop!" cried the donkey. "Don't you see the sun?

Why are you teasing me like this? The rain has stopped! You ought to be ashamed of yourselves!" The animals and birds looked around. The donkey was right. It was a beautiful day. The rain had certainly stopped. They all went off joyfully and left the donkey alone in his corner of the field.

"Next time I sneeze I won't say anything about it" said the grey donkey. "Not a single word. There's no pleasing some people! They all said I was clever, too. Well, maybe I wasn't as clever as I thought I was!"

Next time he sneezed he was *so* surprised to find that no rain came. But *I'm* not surprised – are you?

The Toys Go to the Seaside

Once upon a time the goblin Peeko put his head in at the nursery and cried. "Who wants a day at the seaside?"

The toys sat up with a jerk. They were all alone in the nursery, for Tom and Beryl, whose toys they were, had gone away to stay at their Granny's. The toys were really feeling rather dull. A day at the seaside sounded simply gorgeous!

"How do we go?" asked the pink rabbit.

"By bus," said the goblin grinning. "My bus. I bought it yesterday. Penny each all the way there."

"Ooooh!" said the sailor doll, longingly. "I *would* like to see the sea. I've never been there – and it's dreadful to be a sailor doll and not to know what the sea is like, really it is!"

"Come on, then," said Peeko. "Climb out of the window, all of you. There's plenty of room in the bus."

So the pink rabbit, the sailor doll, the yellow duck, the walking doll, the black dog, and the blue teddy bear all climbed out of the window and got into the goblin's bus, which was standing on the path outside. The goblin took the wheel. The bus gave a roar and a jolt that sent the pink rabbit nearly through the roof – and it was off! It was a fine journey to the sea. The goblin knew all the shortest cuts. It wasn't long before the sailor doll gave a yell and cried, "The sea! The sea!"

"Pooh!" said the goblin. "That's just a duck-pond."

"But aren't those gulls sailing on it?" asked the doll.

"No, *ducks*!" said Peeko.

"Quack, quack!" said the yellow toy duck, and laughed loudly at the sailor doll. After that the doll didn't say anything at all, not even when they came to the real sea and saw it glittering and shining in the sun. He was afraid it might be a duck-pond too – or an extra big puddle!

They all tumbled out of the bus and ran on to the beach. "I'm off for a swim!" said the yellow duck.

"I'd like a sail in a boat!" said the sailor doll. "Oh! There's a nice little boat over there, just my size."

It belonged to a little boy. He had gone home to dinner and had forgotten to take his boat with him. The sailor doll ran to it, pushed it out on to the sea, jumped aboard and was soon enjoying himself!

The pink rabbit thought he would like to make himself a burrow in the sand. It was always difficult to dig a burrow in the nursery. Now he really would be able to dig, and showered sand all over the blue teddy bear.

"Hi, hi, pink rabbit, what are you doing?" cried the bear. But the pink rabbit was already deep in the sandy tunnel, enjoying himself thoroughly, and didn't hear the bear's shout.

"I shall have a nap," said the blue teddy bear. "Don't disturb me, anybody."

He lay down on the soft yellow sand and shut his eyes. Soon a deep growly snore was heard. The black dog giggled and looked at the walking-doll. "Shall we bury him in sand?" he wuffed. "He would be so surprised when he woke up and found himself a sandy bear."

"Yes, let's" said the doll. So they began to bury the sleeping teddy bear in the sand. They piled it over his legs, they piled it over his fat little tummy, they piled it over his arms.

They didn't put any on his head, so all that could be seen of the bear was just his blunt blue snout sticking up. He did look funny.

"I'm off for a walk," said the walking-doll. "This beach is a good place to stretch my legs. I never can walk very far in the nursery – only round and round and round."

She set off over the beach, her long legs twinkling in and out. The black dog was alone. What should he do?

"The sailor doll is sailing. The yellow duck is swimming. The pink rabbit is burrowing. The teddy bear is sleeping. The walking-doll is walking. I think I will go and sniff round for a big fat bone," said the black dog. So off he went.

Now when Peeko the goblin came on the beach two or three hours later, to tell the toys that it was time to go home, do you think he could see a single one? No! There didn't seem to be anyone in sight at all! Peeko was annoyed.

"Just like them to disappear when it's time to go home," he said crossly. "Well, I suppose I must just wait for them, that's all. I'll sit down.

Peeko looked for a nice place to sit. He saw a soft-looking humpy bit of sand. It was really the teddy bear's tummy, buried in the sand, but he didn't know that. He walked over to the humpy bit and sat down in the middle of it.

The blue bear woke up with a jump.

"Oooourrrrrrr," he growled, and sat up suddenly. The goblin fell over in fright. The bear snapped at him and growled again. Then saw it was Peeko.

"What do you mean by sitting down in the middle of me like that?" he said crossly.

"How should I know it was the middle of you when you were all buried in sand?" said Peeko.

"I wasn't," said the bear, in surprise, for he had no idea he had been buried.

"You were," said Peeko.

"I wasn't," said the bear.

"Well, we can go on was-ing and wasn't-ing for ages," said Peeko. Just tell me this, Teddy – where in the world has everyone gone to? It's time to go home."

"Is it really?" said the bear, astonished. "Dear me, it seems as if we've only just come!"

"I don't see why you wanted to come at all if all you do is snore," said Peeko. "Waste of a penny, I call it!"

"Well, if you think that, I won't give you my penny," said the teddy, at once.

"Don't be silly," said the goblin. "Look here, bear, if we don't start soon it will be too late. What am I to do? I'd better go without you."

"Oh no, don't do that," said the bear in alarm. "I'll soon get the others back. We have a special whistle that we use when it's time to go home."

He pursed up his teddy bear mouth and whistled. It was a shrill, loud whistle, and every one of the toys heard it. You should have seen them rushing back to the beach!

The sailor doll sailed his ship proudly to shore, jumped out, and pulled the ship onto the sand. He really did feel a sailor now!

The yellow duck came quacking and swimming in, bobbing up and down in delight. She waddled up the beach, and shook her feathers, sending a shower of drops all over Peeko, who was most annoyed.

The walking-doll tore back across the

sand – and Peeko felt his legs bumped hard, and he sat down very suddenly! The pink rabbit had come out in a great hurry, just between the goblin's legs. The toys laughed till they cried. Peeko was quite angry.

"First I sit on a hump that isn't a hump and get a dreadful fright!" he said. "And then I get bowled over by a silly rabbit who comes out of the sand. Get into the bus all of you, before I say I won't take you home."

They all got into the bus. Most of them were tired and sleepy now, all except the teddy bear, who was very lively indeed – but then, he had been asleep all the time!

They climbed in at the nursery window. They each gave Peeko a penny, and he drove his bus away quietly, and parked it under the lilac bush. The toys crept into the cupboard and sat as still as could be.

And when Tom and Beryl came back the next day from their Granny's they were surprised to see how well and brown their toys all looked.

"Just as if they had been to the sea!" said Tom.

"Don't be silly, Tom!" said Beryl. But he wasn't silly! They *had* been to the sea!

beach. The black dog came running up carrying an enormous bone in his mouth, very old and smelly. The toys looked at it in disgust.

"Where's the pink rabbit?" asked Peeko. "He *would* be last!"

The toys giggled. Peeko was standing at the entrance of the pink rabbit's burrow, but he didn't know he was! The toys knew what would happen – and it did!

The pink rabbit had heard the bear's whistling. He was coming back along his burrow. He suddenly shot out, all legs and

Muzzling the Cat

Once upon a time there lived a big grey cat with orange eyes. He was called Smoky because his fur was the colour of grey smoke. He used to lie on the sunny wall and watch the birds flying about in the trees.

The birds hated Smoky because he was so clever at catching them. He caught their young ones, too, and that made them very miserable. "Let's have a meeting about Smoky," said the thrushes and blackbirds. "Perhaps we can think of some way of stopping his dreadful deeds."

"Friends," said the big blackbird, opening his beautiful orange beak, "we have met here to-day to talk about that horrid cat, Smoky."

At once there was a great deal of twittering and chattering.

"Silence," said the speckled thrush, lifting up one of his feet. Everyone was quiet.

"Smoky catches us and our young ones in a very cruel way," went on the blackbird. "We must stop him. How shall we do this? Has anyone any good ideas?"

So they called a meeting. The robin came, full of woe because one of his youngsters had been caught by Smoky the day before. The wren came, cocking up his perky little tail. The chaffinch came with his pretty salmon-pink breast, and the starling, flashing blue and green in the sunshine. The sparrow was there, too, cheeky as usual, as talkative as the starling.

"Let's all fly round and peck him hard," said the robin, fiercely.

"Well – that would only make him angrier still the next day," said the blackbird. "He would probably kill us all!"

"Let's upset his dish of milk each morning!" cried the wren.

"That's no good!" said the blackbird. "He would be so hungry that he would catch us all the more!"

There was silence for a moment – and then the sparrow and the starling both spoke at once. "Let's-let's-let's…" Then they stopped and glared at one another. They opened their beaks once more. "Let's… let's…"

The starling pecked the sparrow. "Will you be quiet and let *me* speak?" he shouted.

The sparrow pecked at the starling. "You let *me* speak!" he answered back sharply.

"Order, order!" said the thrush sharply. "No quarrelling here!"

"My idea is very good," said the starling hurriedly. "Why not MUZZLE the cat?"

"That was my idea, too!" cried the sparrow in a rage. "I was going to say EXACTLY the same thing!"

"You see," said the starling, taking no notice of the sparrow, "if the cat wears a muzzle, it cannot eat us! There is an old dog's muzzle hanging in the garden shed. We could get that and muzzle the cat well with it."

"A splendid idea," said the blackbird. "Yes, the cat shall be muzzled."

"I thought of it first!" chirrupped the sparrow angrily, trying to peck a feather from the starling's wing.

"You're a story-teller!" squawked the starling. "It was *my* idea!"

"Who is going to do the muzzling?" asked the thrush.

Nobody answered. Nobody wanted *that* little piece of work.

"Come, come," said the blackbird, "*some*body must do it."

"Well, I think it ought to be the one who thought of the idea first," said the thrush firmly.

The starling nearly fell off the tree with fright. The sparrow hid his head under his wing, hoping that nobody would notice he was still there.

"Er… er…" said the starling, at last.

"Well… as the sparrow kept saying just now – it was really *his* idea, not mine. I ought not to have spoken."

The sparrow took his head from beneath his wing in a temper.

"Ho!" he said, "You say it was *my* idea, now you think you've got to muzzle the cat yourself! Well… you can *have* the idea! I don't want it! You said it was yours, and so it is!"

"No quarrelling here!" said the blackbird. "*Both* of you shall do the muzzling together! Sparrow, go and fetch the muzzle from the garden shed."

Off flew the sparrow, and came back with the little wire muzzle in his beak. His smart little mind had thought of an idea to trick the starling.

"Come on, starling!" he cried. "It's no use putting it off. It's got to be done. I'm not a coward, if you are!"

The starling shivered with fright.

"Look," said the sparrow, "I've got the muzzle ready – but I can't muzzle the cat by myself, starling. You must go and hold him still whilst I put it on. Come on!"

The starling gave a great splutter of fright. Hold that cat still! Oooooh! The very thought made the starling feel quite faint.

"Do hurry up!" chirrupped the sparrow. "Smoky is lying on the wall. Just fly down and hold him tightly by the neck. Then, as soon as he is quite still, I will slip the muzzle over his mouth."

"Yes, hurry and help the sparrow!" cried all the other birds to the frightened starling.

But he didn't dare to. He spread his wings and flew squawking and spluttering away, leaving the sparrow and the muzzle behind him.

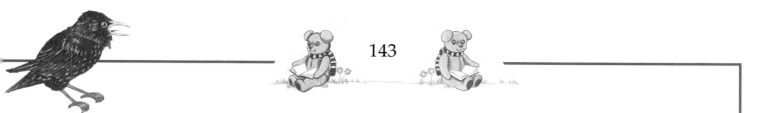

"Coward! Coward!" cried all the birds.

The sparrow was delighted. "Come along, somebody," he cried. "I don't mind who holds the cat still for me. Will *you*, blackbird?"

"I've got to go back to see my wife," said the blackbird, in a hurry, and he flew off. And before very long the sparrow was left quite alone, chuckling and chirrupping to himself in delight.

Then he heard a voice from below him that made him tremble with fear.

"Ho, little sparrow, I heard all that has been said," said Smoky the cat, with a laugh. "How cowardly all the birds are except you, aren't they? Well, you shall show them how brave you are! I promise to keep quite still, and you shall try to muzzle me. So come down and do what you want to!"

But alas! The sparrow had fled! The muzzle had dropped down to the ground, and Smoky yawned widely showing his sharp white teeth.

"A fuss about nothing!" he said. "They are all as cowardly as each other. I shall go and get my bread and milk."

Have you ever heard the starlings talking loudly to one another, or the sparrows twittering in a crowd among the trees? You'll know what they are talking about now… how the cat was NEARLY muzzled – but not quite!

The Ho-Ho Goblins

Once upon a time the Ho-Ho goblins laid a plan. They wanted to catch the Skippetty pixies, but for a long time they hadn't been able even to get near them. Now they had thought of a marvellous idea!

"Listen!" said Snicky, the head goblin. "You know when the pixies sit down to feast, in the middle of their dancing, don't you? Well, they sit on toadstools! And if *we* grow those toadstools we can put a spell in them so that as soon as the pixies sit down on them, they shoot through the earth into our caves below – and we shall have captured them very nicely indeed!"

"A splendid idea!" said the other goblins in delight. "We'll do it!"

"Leave it all to me," said Snicky. "I will go to them and offer to grow them toadstools for their dance much more cheaply than anyone else – and I will grow them just over our caves, as I said – then the rest is easy."

So the goblins left it to Snicky. As soon as he heard that the invitations to the party had been sent out, he went knocking at the door of Pinky, one of the chief pixies.

"What do you want?" asked Pinky, opening the door. She did not like the Ho-Ho goblins.

"Dear Madam Pinky," said Snicky, bowing low, "I come to ask you if you will kindly allow me to grow the toadstools for you for your dance."

"How much do you charge?" asked Pinky.

"One gold piece for one hundred toadstools," said Snicky.

"That is very cheap," said Pinky. "We had to pay three gold pieces last time."

"Madam, they will be excellent toadstools, strong and beautiful," said Snicky. "Please let the Ho-Ho goblins do them for you."

"Well, I don't like the goblins, but that's no reason why I shouldn't have their toadstools," said Pinky. "Very well. You shall make them for our dance. We want them in the wood under the oak tree."

"Madam, it is very damp there," said Snicky.

"It would be better to grow them under the birch tree."

Snicky knew quite well that under the birch tree lay the caves of the Ho-Ho goblins. He must grow the toadstools there, or the goblins would not be able to capture the pixies as they had planned.

"Oh, very well," said Pinky. "It can't make much difference whether the dance is held under the oak or the birch. We want the toadstools on the next full-moon night, Snicky."

Snicky ran off full of glee. He had got what he wanted! He called a meeting of the others, and told them.

"Now," he said, "not one of you must tell a word of this to anyone, for we must keep it a secret. We must get a runaway spell from Witch Grumple, and each toadstool must be rubbed with the spell. Then, at a magic word, all the toadstools, with the pixies on them, will rush away through the ground straight to our caves below."

"Hurrah!" cried the Ho-Ho goblins. "They will be our servants at last."

Snicky went to ask Witch Grumple for the spell. She was not at home. Her servant, a big black cat with green eyes, said that his mistress had gone walking through the fields to collect some dew shining in the new moon.

"I'll go and meet her," said Snicky. So off he went. He found the witch walking by the hedges that ran round the ripening cornfield. She had a dish in which she was collecting the silvery dewdrops.

"Good evening, Witch Grumple," said Snicky. "May I speak secretly with you for a moment?"

"Certainly," said the witch. She looked all around to see that no-one was about. "Come into the corn," she said. "No-one will hear us then. What is it you want?"

"I want a runaway spell," said Snicky.

"What will you give me for it?" asked the witch.

"I'll give you two Skippetty pixies for servants," said Snicky.

"Don't be silly," said Grumple. "You haven't any pixies to give away!"

"I soon shall have, if you let me have the runaway spell," said Snicky.

"Tell me what you are going to do with it," said Grumple.

"No," said Snicky; "someone might hear me,"

"There is no-one to hear you," said Grumple. "Tell me, or I will not let you have the spell."

So Snicky told Grumple exactly what hewas going to do to capture the pixies, and she shook with laughter.

"Splendid!" she said. "I shall be glad to see those stuck-up little pixies punished. Come back with me and I'll give you the spell."

Now all would have gone well with the Ho-Ho goblins' plan – if someone hadn't overheard the secret that Snicky told Grumple. Who heard it? You will never guess.

The corn heard it with its many, many ears! Grumple had quite forgotten that corn has ears. They were ripe ears, too, ready to catch the slightest whisper. They listened to all that Snicky said, and, because they liked the Skippetty pixies, they wanted to warn them. So the next time the wind blew the corn, it whispered its secret to the breeze.

"Shish-a-shish-a-shish-a-shish!" went the corn as the wind blew over it. The wind understood its language and listened in astonishment to the tale the corn told of Snicky's plan. Off it went to the pixies at once.

When Pinky heard of Snicky's plan, she went pale with rage and fear. To think how that horrid, horrid goblin had nearly tricked her! Off she sped to the Fairy King and told him everything. He laughed and said, "Aha! Now we shall be able to play a nice little trick on Snicky himself!"

So, on the night of the dance, all the pixies laughed and talked as if they had no idea of the toadstool trick. The goblins crept around, watching and waiting for the moment when they could send the toadstools rushing down below to their caves.

Suddenly Pinky stopped the dance and said, "Let's play musical chairs for a change! Goblins, come and play with us!"

The Ho-Ho goblins felt flattered that they should be asked to play with the pixies. So they all came running up. Pinky pointed to the toadstools that Snicky had grown for them.

The band began again. Pixies and goblins ran merrily round the toadstools – but every pixie had been warned not to

sit down, but to let the goblins take the toadstools. So, when the music stopped, the goblins made a rush for the toadstools and sat heavily down on them meaning to win the game of musical chairs.

As soon as Pinky saw the goblins sitting on the toadstools, she called out a magic word at the top of her voice. Those toadstools sank down through the ground at top speed! You see, Snicky had rubbed them hard with the runaway spell the night before – and Pinky knew the word to set them off!

To the goblins' great fright, the toadstools rushed down to their cave – and there, calmly waiting for them, were the soldiers of the Fairy King. As the toadstools came to rest in the caves, each goblin was surrounded by three soldiers. They were prisoners!

"That was a fine trick you planned, wasn't it?" grinned a soldier. "But not so fine when it's played on yourselves! Come along now, quick march!"

Off the goblins went – and for a whole year they had to work hard for the pixies, to punish them for trying to play such a horrid trick.

And to this day they don't know who gave their secret away

– although people say that if you listen to the corn as it whispers in the wind, you can, if you have sharp ears, hear it telling the wind all about Witch Grumple and Snicky the goblin. I'd love to hear it, wouldn't you?

Poor Captain Puss!

Ronald and Jill were very lucky. In the summer they always went to Cliffsea, where their father had a house almost on the beach. It was such fun to wake up in the morning and hear the waves splashing on the sands not far off.

All the household went to Cliffsea in the summer, even Toby the dog and Patter the kitten! No-one was left behind. Toby liked the sea very much, and Patter loved playing about in the sand.

Next door to the children's house was a smaller one, and two cats and a dog lived there with their mistress. The dog was called Spot, and the cats were called Sooty and Snowball. So you can guess what they were like to look at.

Toby, Patter, Sooty, Snowball, and Spot were soon good friends. Patter the kitten had a fine time with them. They made quite a fuss of her because she was the smallest and youngest.

So she was rather spoilt, and she became vain and boastful. Ronald and Jill spoilt her, too, and said she was just the cleverest kitten they had ever seen.

"See how she runs after my ball!" said Ronald, as Patter raced over the sand to get his ball.

"See how Patter plays with this bit of seaweed!" said Jill. "She fetched it off the rocks for me, Ronald. She *is* a clever kitten! She can do simply anything."

Patter felt very clever indeed. She went about with her head in the air and began to think that the other animals were rather stupid.

But there was one thing she would not do! She wouldn't go paddling and bathing with the children as Toby and Spot did. No – she hated the water. She thought it was simply horrid to get her dainty little feet wet.

Then one day Ronald and Jill bought down a beautiful big ship to the beach. It was a toy one, but was so big that Toby and Spot could almost get into it. Ronald and Jill played happily with it all morning, and sailed it on the rock-pools that were spread all over the beach.

When they went indoors to dinner the five animals crowded round the pretty boat.

"I wish I could sail in it!" said Toby. "I'd love to sail over that pool. I would make a good captain!"

"So would I," said Spot, wagging his tail and sniffing at the boat as it stood half upright in the sand.

"I would make the *best* captain!" said Patter the kitten boastfully. "Ronald and Jill are always saying what a clever kitten I am. I am sure I could sail this ship much better than any of you!"

"Why, Patter, you little story-teller!" cried Snowball. "You know how you hate to get your feet wet! You wouldn't be any good at all at sailing a boat."

"Yes, I should," said Patter crossly. "I know just what to do. You pull that thing there – the tiller, it's called – and the boat goes this way and that. I heard Ronald say so!"

"You don't know anything about it at all," said Sooty scornfully. "You are just showing off as usual!"

"I'm not!" mewed Patter angrily. She jumped into the boat and put her paw on the tiller. "There you are," she said. "This is what makes the boat go!"

The others laughed at her. They were sure that Patter would hate to go sailing really. They ran off and left her. She stared after them crossly, and then she lay down in the boat in the warm sunshine. She wouldn't go and play with the others if they were going to be so horrid to her. No, they could just play by themselves!

Patter shut her eyes, for the sun was very bright. She put her nose on her paws and slept. She didn't hear the sea coming closer and closer. She didn't know the tide was coming in! It crept up to the boat. It shook it a little. But Patter slept on, dreaming of sardines and cream.

Toby, Spot, Sooty and Snowball wondered where Patter was. They couldn't see her curled up in the ship. They thought she had gone indoors in a huff.

"She is getting to be a very foolish little kitten," said Toby. "We must not take so much notice of her."

"It is silly of her to pretend that she would make such a good sailor," said Sooty. "Everyone knows that cats hate the water."

"Well, we won't bother about her any more," said Snowball. "She's just a little silly. Let's lie down behind this shady rock and have a snooze. I'm sleepy."

So they all lay down and slept. They were far away from the tide and were quite safe.

But Patter was anything but safe! The sea was all round the ship now! In another minute it would be floating! A great big wave came splashing up the beach – and the ship floated! There it was, quite upright, floating beautifully!

The rock-pool disappeared. It was now part of the big sea. The ship sailed merrily on it. It bobbed up and down on the waves.

Patter suddenly woke up, and wondered why things bobbed about so. She sat up and saw that she had fallen asleep in the boat – and when she looked over the side, what a shock for her! She was sailing on the sea! Big waves came and went under the boat. The beach was far away!

"Miaow!" wailed Patter. "Miaow! I'm out at sea! I'm afraid! I shall drown!"

But no-one heard her. The sea was making such a noise as the tide came in. Patter forgot how she had boasted about being a good sailor. She forgot that she had boasted she could sail the boat quite well. She just clung on to the side and watched with frightened eyes as the green waves came and went.

Ronald and Jill suddenly remembered that they had left their sailing ship on the beach.

"My goodness! And the tide's coming in!" said Ronald in dismay. "Quick, Jill, we must go and see if our boat is safe!"

They ran from the house to the beach – and then saw the tide was right in. And, far away, on the big waves, floated their beautiful ship, all by itself!

"Look!" cried Jill. "There it is! But there is someone in it. Who is it, Ronald?"

Ronald stared hard. Then he shouted out in surprise: "Why, it's Patter the kitten! Yes, it really is! Look at her in the boat Jill!"

"Oh, the clever thing!" cried Jill, who really thought the kitten was sailing the ship. "Oh, whoever heard of a kitten sailing a boat before? Spot, Toby, come and look at Patter sailing our ship!"

Spot, Toby, Sooty and Snowball awoke in a hurry and ran to see what all the excitement was about. When they saw Patter the kitten out in the boat, rocking up and down on the sea, they could hardly believe their eyes.

"Captain Puss is sailing the boat," said Jill. "Captain Patter Puss! Isn't she clever?"

But Spot didn't think that Patter was as clever as all that. His sharp ears had caught a tiny mew – and that mew was very, very frightened. It wasn't the voice of a bold captain – it was the mew of a terrified kitten!

"I believe she went to sleep in the boat and the tide came and took it away," wuffed Spot to Toby.

"Well, it will do her good to see that she isn't such a marvellous captain after all!" Toby barked back.

"She *would* be silly enough to fall asleep just when the tide was coming in," said Sooty.

"All the same, she's very frightened," said Snowball, who had heard two or three frightened mews.

"Sail the boat to shore, Patter!" shouted Ronald.

"Sail her in! We don't want to lose her!"

But Patter was much too frightened to pay any attention to what was said. She just went on clinging to the side of the boat. She felt very ill, and wished that she was on dry land.

Spot was quite worried. He knew what a little silly Patter really was – but all the same he thought she had been frightened quite enough. What could be done?

"I'll go and fetch her," wuffed Spot, and he plunged into the sea. He swam strongly through the waves, which were now getting quite big, for the wind had blown up in the afternoon. Up and down went Spot, swimming as fast as he could, for he was really rather afraid that the ship might be blown over in the wind – and then what would happen to Patter!

The boat was a good way out. The wind blew the white sails strongly. The waves bobbed it up and down like a cork. Patter was terribly frightened, for once or twice she thought the boat was going over.

And just as Spot got there, the wind gave the sails such a blow that the boat *did* go over! Smack! The sails hit the sea, and the boat lay on its side. Splash! Poor Patter was thrown into the water. She couldn't swim – but Spot was there just in time! He caught hold of her by the skin of her neck and, holding her head above the water, he swam back to the shore. The ship lay far out to sea on its side.

Spot put poor, wet, cold Patter on the sand, and shook himself. Patter mewed weakly.

The others came running up to her,

"Well, you didn't make such a good sailor after all," said Sooty.

"Don't say unkind things now," said Snowball. "Patter has been punished enough. Come into the house, Patter, and sit by the kitchen fire and dry yourself."

Ronald and Jill watched the five animals running into the house. Then Ronald turned up his shorts and went wading into the water to see if he could get back his boat.

"That kitten was silly!" he said. "She took my boat out to sea, couldn't sail it back again, made it flop on to its side, and fell out herself! She isn't so clever as she thinks."

He got back his boat and went to dry the sails in the kitchen. Patter was there, sitting as close to the fire as she could, getting dry.

"Hullo, Captain Puss!" said Ronald. "I don't think you are much of a sailor!"

"No, she is just a dear, silly little kitten," said Jill.

Patter felt ashamed. How she wished she hadn't boasted about being a good sailor! She wondered if the others would ever speak to her again.

They did, of course, and as soon as they found that she wasn't boastful any more they were as good friends as ever.

But if Patter forgets, they laugh and say, "Now, Captain Patter! Would you like to go sailing again?"

Goldie and the Toys

Once there was a canary in a cage. The bird was as yellow as gold, so he was called Goldie. He belonged to Eric and Hilda, and they were very fond of him; they cleaned out his cage every day and gave him fresh food and water.

Now every night he used to watch the toys come alive and play with one another. He would peep out of his cage with his bright black eyes and long to get out and play with the dolls and animals. They had such good times.

"Do open my cage door and let me out!" he would beg each night. "I want to dance with the curly-haired doll! I want to ride in that big train! I want to wind up the musical boxand hear it sing. Oh, do let me out, toys!"

But they wouldn't, for they knew that he might escape out of the nursery, and then Eric and Hilda would be very sad. So they shook their heads and went on playing by themselves.

But one night, after Christmas, there was a new toy in the nursery. This was a green duck, and it liked the look of the yellow canary very much. So when the little bird began to call out to the toys to let it out of its cage, the duck spoke up.

"Why don't we let the canary out to have a bit of fun with us? After all, the poor thing is stuck in its cage all day long and never gets a chance to play a game. I'd like to be friends with it. I'm a bird, too, and I should like a good long chat with another bird."

"Yes, yes!" cried the canary eagerly. "Let me out, duck! I am so lonely up here! I should love a chat with a beautiful bird like you!"

"The windows and the door are shut," said the big doll. "I don't see that it will do any harm. The canary couldn't escape out of the room if it wanted to!"

"I don't want to escape!" cried the canary. "I just want to have a game. I will go back to my cage when everything is over."

"Very well," said the biggest doll. "You shall come out and join us this evening – but remember, if you don't behave properly, we'll never let you out again!"

The canary promised to be good, and the toy clown threw a rope up to the cage, and then climbed right up to it. He opened the door and out flew Goldie, simply delighted to stretch his wings and have a fly round.

You should have seen how Goldie enjoyed himself. The toys set the musical box going and when the tune was tinkled out the canary took hold of the curly-haired doll with his wing and off they danced together over the nursery floor. The canary really danced very well indeed, for he was so light on his feet.

After they had had a good dance, the clockwork train offered to take the toys for a ride. Of course, the canary wanted to drive, and, my goodness me, he drove so fast that the train couldn't see where it was going, and bumped into a chair leg. Out fell all the toys in a heap, and they were not very pleased with the canary. He didn't get bumped at all because as soon as he saw the engine was going to run into the chair leg he simply spread his wings and flew safely into the air!

Then the toys played
hide-and-seek, and the
canary liked that very much
because he could fly up to the top of
the curtains, or on to the clock, and
no toys thought of looking there for him,
so he was the only one that was never
caught. He did enjoy himself.

At last cockcrow came, when all the
toys had to go back to the toy-cupboard
and sleep.

"It's time to go back to your cage,
Goldie," said the big doll; "You've had a
lovely time, haven't you? Just fly back
to your cage now, there's a good bird,
and let the clockwork clown shut
your door."

"Not I!" said Goldie cheekily. "I'm not
going back to my cage for hours and
HOURS and HOURS. No, I'm going to
stay in the nursery and fly about as long
as I like!"

"But you promised!" cried the toys.

"I don't care!" said the naughty canary.

"How dreadful to break a promise!" said the green duck, who was feeling hurt because the canary had hardly spoken a word to him. "I wonder you're not ashamed of yourself. Go back to your cage at once."

But the canary simply wouldn't. He just flew away as soon as any toy came near him. It was most annoying.

"We shall have to do *something*!" said the big doll in despair. "If we leave him loose like this he will fly out of the door in the morning when the housemaid opens it, and then the cat will get him! What *can* we do?"

They all whispered together, and then at last the clockwork clown had an idea.

"Let's spread the table in the dolls' house, and say we're going to have supper there," he said. "The canary will want to join us, of course – and we'll get him in. Then we'll all go out and slam the door. He will have to stay in the dolls' house till morning then."

"Splendid idea!" cried all the toys. They ran to the dolls' house, and began to lay the cloth. They set out the tiny cups, saucers and plates, and then the big doll fetched some sweets from the toy sweet-shop.

"What are you doing?" cried the canary from his perch on a candlestick.

"We're going to have supper," said the clockwork clown.

"Well, I'm coming, too," said the canary.

Down he flew and hopped in at the front door of the dolls' house. The curly-haired doll saw that all the windows were tightly shut, and the clockwork clown stuffed up the chimney with paper so that Goldie couldn't escape that way.

The canary sat down on a chair, and the big doll gave him a sweet on his plate. He

put it into his beak, and didn't notice that one by one all the toys were creeping out of the house. At last he was quite alone.

Slam! The canary jumped up in fright. The door of the dolls' house was tight shut. He was caught.

"Let me out, let me out!" he yelled.

"No," said the toys. "You just stay here!"

"Let me go back to my cage," said the canary.

"No, " said the big doll at once. "As soon as we open the door you would fly away again!"

"I promise I would go back to my cage," said Goldie, pecking the front door with his beak.

"We don't trust you," said the clown. "You broke your promise before, so we are sure you would break it again." Then the toys went to the toy cupboard and fell asleep. The canary hopped on the table of the dolls' house and went to sleep too.

In the morning Eric and Hilda came into the nursery – and the first thing they saw was the open door of the canary's cage. How upset they were!

"Goldie's gone, Goldie's gone!" they cried, "Oh, where can he be?"

Goldie heard his name and he hopped about excitedly in the dolls' house, trilling loudly.

"Listen!" said Eric, astonished. "Can you hear Goldie trilling? Where is he?"

"It sounds as if he were in the dolls' house!" said Hilda, astonished. They knelt down and peeped through the window – and there they saw Goldie, hopping about inside the little house.

"There he is!" said Eric. "But however did he get there? What a funny thing! He can't have got in there and shut the door himself!"

The children opened the door and Eric slipped in his hand and took hold of Goldie very gently – and in two seconds the little canary was safely in his cage once more, singing very loudly indeed.

"I'm sure our big doll is smiling," said Hilda suddenly. "I wonder why?"

"Perhaps she could tell us how Goldie got into the dolls' house!" said Eric.

She certainly could, couldn't she? You may be quite sure that the toys *never* let Goldie out of his cage again. He really was much too naughty to be trusted!

Mrs. Dilly's Duck

Mrs. Dilly had a pet duck. It was large and white and fat, and its name was Jemima. It had a pond all to itself in the garden, and it was very fond of Mrs. Dilly.

One day, when Mrs. Dilly had two friends to tea – Peter Penny and Sally Simple – she told them about her pet duck.

"She's a wonderful creature," she said proudly. "She comes when she's called, and she can shake or nod her head when you ask her questions!"

"Good gracious!" said Peter Penny.

"Call her now," said Sally Simple.

"Jemima, Jemima, Jemima!" cried Mrs. Dilly. The duck was swimming on the pond, but she heard Mrs. Dilly's voice. She swam to the edge, climbed out, waddled down the path and in at the door.

"Quack-quack!" she said.

"Oh, you clever thing," said Peter Penny.

"Do you love your mistress?" said Sally Simple.

Jemima nodded her feathery head twice.

"Do you like worms?" asked Peter Penny.

Jemima nodded her head hard. "Quack, quack, quack!" she said excitedly.

"Would you like to come home with me?" asked Sally Simple.

Jemima shook her head six times. She was much too fond of Mrs. Dilly to want to leave her.

"You're a dear, clever thing!" said Peter Penny, and he held out half of his cake to Jemima. The duck had never tasted cake before and she took it in her beak and gobbled it down eagerly. "Quack" she said, looking up for more. "Quack!"

Sally Simple gave her a bit of bread and butter with raspberry jam on it. Jemima gobbled it up. Ooooh! It was good! Then Mrs. Dilly laughed and held out a ginger biscuit. Jemima gobbled that too. This was better than worms, and better than frogs!

"Now, that's enough," said Mrs. Dilly. "Off you go back to the pond, Jemima." But the duck didn't want to go. It was nice to be made a fuss of, and how she loved the cake and biscuits and bread and butter! She rubbed her soft head against Peter Penny's knee, and he stroked her.

"Do sell her to me any time you are tired of her," said Peter Penny.

"Or to me," said Sally Simple. "I'd love to have a duck like this!"

Mrs. Dilly shooed Jemima out of the warm kitchen and shut the door. "I don't expect I'd ever want to part with her," she said.

Now Jemima the duck had been so excited over her petting and the titbits she had had, that the next day she thought she would go to the kitchen again and see if there were any more treats to be had. So she left the pond and waddled to the kitchen. The door was open. Jemima went in. Mrs. Dilly had just washed over the floor and it was clean and shining. Jemima's feet were muddy and wet. They left dirty marks all over the floor.

Jemima stood on her toes and looked on the table. There was a cake there, just baked. Jemima took two or three pecks at it. It was very good.

Just then Mrs. Dilly came bustling into the kitchen. When she saw her nice clean floor all marked by Jemima's dirty feet she was very angry. But she was even angrier when she saw her new cake pecked to bits!

"Oh, you naughty duck! Oh, you rascally creature!" she cried, clapping her hands at Jemima and shooing her to the door. "Don't you ever do this again!"

But you know, once Jemima had found what a pleasant place the kitchen was, always with something good in the larder or on the table, she used to waddle there every day. Mrs. Dilly tried to remember to keep the door shut, but she hadn't a very good memory, and every time she left it open, Jemima was sure to waddle in!

The things that naughty duck ate! A string of sausages, a cherry-pie, a pound of chocolate biscuits, and even a large cucumber! Mrs. Dilly got crosser and crosser.

"Now, Jemima, the very next time you come in here, dirtying my kitchen and stealing my food, I shall take you to Peter Penny," she said.

But that afternoon what did she do but leave her door open again, and of course in waddled Jemima and gobbled up a jam tart in the larder!

Mrs. Dilly was very cross. She put on her shawl and hat, tied a string round Jemima's leg, and set off to get the train to Peter Penny's. Jemima was miserable, but she had to go.

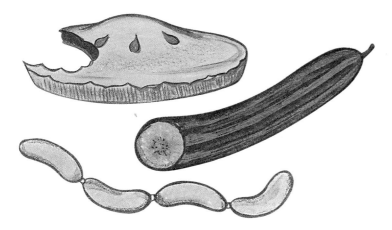

Mrs. Dilly took a ticket for herself and one for Jemima. Then she bought a paper and sat down on a seat to wait for the train. She tied Jemima's string to the seat.

Soon, with a roar and a clatter, the train came in. Jemima was frightened and went under the seat. Mrs. Dilly folded her paper, thinking hard about what she had been reading, and ran to the train. She forgot all about Jemima!

She got into the carriage and the train went off. Mrs. Dilly read her paper again. She got out at the next station and set off for Peter Penny's house. Peter was in the garden, working.

"Good-day," he said to Mrs. Dilly.

"What have you come along here for?"

"I've brought my duck for you," said Mrs. Dilly. "She's such a nuisance, dirtying my kitchen and stealing food.

"Oh, good!" said Peter Penny, "Where is she?"

Mrs. Dilly looked round for Jemima – but, of course, she wasn't there! She was still in the station!

"Bless us all!" cried Mrs. Dilly. "I've left her by the station seat. How forgetful I am! I must go back and bring her another day."

Well, when she had journeyed back by train to her own station, there was no duck there! Jemima had got tired of hearing trains thundering in and out of the station and had pecked her string in half. Then she had waddled solemnly home, quacking to herself all the way.

"This is too bad, Jemima, too bad!" cried Mrs. Dilly, almost in tears. She took a broom and swept the surprised duck out of the kitchen. "I'll take you to Peter Penny to-morrow as sure as my name is Dilly."

So the next morning Mrs. Dilly tied the string round Jemima's leg one more and hurried to the station. She did not even sit down on the seat this time, in case she forgot Jemima again. She jumped into the train and Jemima had to go too. The frightened duck crept under the seat and lay there whilst the train rumbled on. She was too afraid even to quack.

When she got back to her garden she had seen that the kitchen door was open as usual. So when Mrs. Dilly arrived back in a flurry, wondering wherever her poor duck had gone to, she found Jemima standing on the kitchen rug, her head tucked into her wing, fast asleep – and the lettuces, tomatoes, and radishes were all missing out of the larder!

door to give up her ticket. Then off she went to Peter Penny's.

But she had forgotten Jemima again. The duck was still hiding under the carriage seat. She did not dare to come out. She stayed there till the engine was shunted to the back of the train, ready to go off home once more, for this station was the last one on the line. The train clattered off. When it stopped at Jemima's own station the duck waddled out from under the seat.

Someone opened the door. Jemima jumped out as the passenger was getting in – what a shock he got to see a large duck struggling by him! Jemima gave an anxious quack and waddled out of the station gate. She set off for home.

As for Mrs. Dilly, she soon arrived at Peter Penny's again. "I've brought Jemima as I promised," she said.

"Good!" said Peter Penny. "Bring her in." But there was no duck there to bring in!

Mrs. Dilly nodded her head and slept. When the train drew up at the station the porter put his head in at the window and bawled loudly: "Change here! Change here!"

Mrs. Dilly woke with a jump. She bundled herself out and, rubbing her sleepy eyes, went to the station

"Lawkamussy, I've left her in the train this time!" said Mrs. Dilly, and she hurried back to the station. But the train had gone, so she had to catch the next, worrying all the time about where Jemima had gone.

But she needn't have worried, for Jemima was safely in the kitchen, gobbling up all the flowers out of the vases. Really, you never knew what the duck was going to eat next!

When Mrs. Dilly got home she was very angry indeed. "I'll take you to Sally Simple's this very afternoon!" she scolded. "I don't like to go to Peter's again, for he will laugh at me – but I'll take you to Sally's and leave you there, as sure as there is butter on bread."

So that afternoon once more Jemima had a string tied to her leg and once more she set off down the road, this time to Sally Simple's. They didn't go by train, because Sally's was not very far away. They went through the park, where the children were playing, Jemima following solemnly, waddling on her flat feet.

Mrs. Dilly's shoe-lace came undone. She stopped near some railings, and tied Jemima's string there. There were other strings tied there too – the strings of kites flying high in the air. It was a windy day and the children in the park had brought out their kites. Once they had them high in the air they had tied the strings safely to the railing, so that the kites might fly high, whilst they went off to play ball.

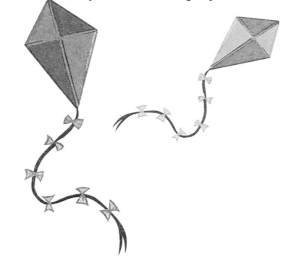

Mrs. Dilly tied up her shoe. Then she untied a string from the railing and set off. But dear old Mrs. Dilly didn't look to see that her string was the right one – and she had untied a kite-string! So off she went, very solemnly, with a kite flying high in the air behind her! How everyone stared!

Sally Simple lived just near the park. Mrs. Dilly went down a street, still flying the kite without knowing it, and knocked at Sally's door.

"Who's there?" cried Sally. "I'm just doing my hair."

"It's Mrs. Dilly," said Mrs. Dilly. "I've brought my bad duck to you. I don't want her anymore."

"Bring her in, then – bring her in," said Sally, and she opened the door, with her hair down her back. How she stared when she saw the kite flying behind Mrs. Dilly.

"Why are you flying a kite?" she asked.

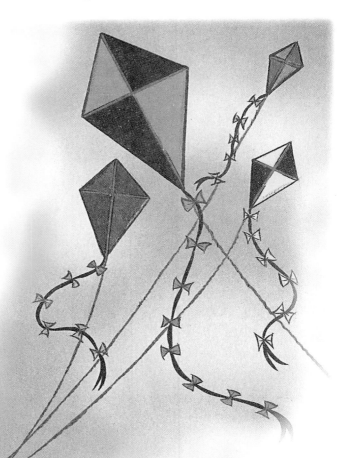

"I'm *not* flying a kite!" said Mrs. Dilly, amazed. She looked round for Jemima – and to her enormous astonishment saw that the string went up into the air!

"It must be that Jemima has flown up high in the sky," she said, pulling at the kite. "It can't be a kite, Sally. It must be Jemima flying up there – and yet she didn't have such a long string."

Sally pulled at the string and the kite came down. "It's a kite, Mrs Dilly," said

Sally. "Well, it's a funny thing that a duck can turn into a kite, but there it is – it seems to have happened!"

Mrs. Dilly was so puzzled that she didn't even remember to say good-bye. She turned and went home, leaving the kite behind her, where it was found by its owner a little while afterwards. Of course Mrs. Dilly didn't find Jemima in the park, for someone had untied the duck and she had waddled home thankfully. When Mrs. Dilly got home she saw Jemima eating the apples out of the fruit dish.

"It seems that I'm not to get rid of you after all, Jemima," said Mrs. Dilly sadly. "I must put up with you. If only I could remember to shut my back door every-thing would be quite all right! Oh – I know what I'll do! I'll get a cat – and then you will be too frightened to come into the kitchen any more!"

So she got a big white cat called Snowy, and it sat in front of the kitchen fire and warmed its toes. At first Jemima was much too scared to come indoors – but do you know what she is doing now? She is making friends with Snowy the cat, and in no time at all she'll be into the kitchen again, gobbling up all the food in the larder – and I shouldn't be surprised if Snowy doesn't help her! Poor Mrs. Dilly! I wonder what she'll do then, don't you?

Off to the Moon!

The pixie Tiptoe was most annoyed with her small servant, Woffles the mouse. He wouldn't do his work, and he had grumbled because there was only bacon rind for his breakfast, and he wanted cheese.

"Woffles, I can't think what is the matter with you," said Tiptoe. "You used to be so happy and hard-working. Now you grumble all day long, and turn up your nose at the nice things I give you to eat."

"I want cheese," said Woffles sulkily.

"But too much cheese isn't good for you," said Tiptoe. "Besides, I can't keep buying the best cheese for you. I don't even have it myself!"

"I shall leave you and go to work for someone else then," said Woffles, taking off his apron and folding it up.

"Who will you work for?" asked Tiptoe.

"I don't know of anyone else who wants a servant. All the fairies and the pixies have their own mice, cats or rabbits."

"I shall go to work for the man in the moon," said Woffles, packing his bag. "I hear the moon is made of green cheese. That will suit me very well. I shall take a nibble of it whenever I like."

Tiptoe began to laugh. "Don't be silly, Woffles," she said. "You will never get to the moon! Stay with me and be a sensible little mouse. I am very fond of you and should miss you if you went!"

But Woffles would not stay. He put on his hat, took up his bag, said good-bye and went. Tiptoe watched him go, shaking her head, for she knew he would never get to the moon.

Woffles wandered here and there, asking his way to the moon, but no-one seemed to know it. They laughed and shook their heads.

"The moon is made of green cheese," said the little mouse. "I am very anxious to go there and work for the man in the moon. He would feed me well, I know!"

Now Tiptoe missed her little mouse, for she was very fond of him. She wondered where he was, and soon found that he was still wandering about, asking the way to the moon. She heard that he was looking thin, for he had had very little to eat. She was sorry for him, but she knew that he would not come back to her until he was sure he could not find the moon. He was a very obstinate little mouse.

So she planned to play a trick on him. She went to her cousin, Pointy, and with much laughter they planned the trick. Her cousin's pointed ears twitched with delight, and he promised to do all that Tiptoe wanted.

He was to buy a green balloon from the toy shop, and blow it up until it was simply enormous. Then he was to hang it on the roof of his house, tied tightly to the chimney so that it looked like the moon in the sky! Woffles would be sure to see it when he came that way, and would think that Pointy was the man in the moon!

Then Pointy would say no, he didn't want a servant, and Woffles would sigh and go back to Tiptoe. It was all very simple!

Pointy bought the balloon and blew it up till it was bigger than he was! He got a ladder and climbed up it with the balloon. He tied it tightly to the chimney – and

there it was, shining green in the sky, looking for all the world like the moon!

That day Woffles came along, still carrying his bag, and looking for the man in the moon. When he saw the big balloon away up in the sky he was overjoyed.

"The moon at last!" he cried. "And it is green, too, now that I see it close to! It must be made of cheese after all! I will look for the man who belongs to it, at once!"

He hadn't far to look. Pointy was in the garden, and how he grinned when he saw Woffles coming along.

"I'm so glad to find you," said Woffles. "I have looked for the moon for a long time. I want to be your servant."

"Dear me, I'm really very sorry, but I'm afraid I don't want a servant," said Pointy.

"Oh, but I'm a *very* good one!" said Woffles. "I can cook, bake, sweep, wash, dust, scrub and lay the table. I can–"

"Very nice indeed – but I don't *want* a servant," said Pointy. "You had better go back to where you came from. Jobs are hard to get these days."

Woffles was bitterly disappointed.

"I'm so fond of cheese!" he said. "I thought if I was your servant I could have a nibble of the moon now and then. I know it is made of green cheese."

"Well, that's the first time *I* heard the moon is made of cheese!" said Pointy laughing. "Now go home, little mouse. Go back to your kind mistress."

Woffles turned away sadly. Pointy went indoors, chuckling. Now Tiptoe would soon have her servant back again!

The little mouse looked longingly at the green balloon up in the sky. It did really look like cheese to him, for he had quite made up his mind that it *was* cheese and nothing *but* cheese!

I'll just climb up that ladder, and have a small nibble!" he thought suddenly. "I'm very hungry. I could do with a nice bit of green cheese!"

He put down his bag, ran to the ladder and climbed up it to the roof. He ran up the chimney and then cleverly clung on to the string that the balloon flew from.

He took a bite – and oh, stars and moon and sun! The moon went POP! Yes, it did! It burst to bits and Woffles fell down the chimney right into the pot of cold water that Pointy had just put on to boil! He jumped out, shivering and shaking and Pointy stared at him in great astonishment.

"I bit the moon – and it burst!" stammered poor Woffles. "It's gone! Oh, what shall I do? Oh, why did I leave my darling mistress Tiptoe? Oh, what a fright I got!"

Pointy ran outside and saw the burst balloon on the roof. How he laughed! Poor little mouse, he *must* have got a fright! He ran indoors again.

"Listen, Woffles," he said. "You've spoilt my moon – and as you know now, it *wasn't* made of green cheese – but if you like to go back to Tiptoe, tell her you are sorry for leaving her, and work hard again for her, I'll forgive you and say nothing more about it!"

"Oh, you *are* kind!" wept Woffles, picking up his bag that he had left in the garden. "I'll go back at once. I'll never leave Tiptoe again!"

So back he went, and is with Tiptoe to this very day. When next he saw the moon sailing in the sky, he was very pleased.

"So the man in the moon has got a new moon now!" he said to himself. "I hope nobody bursts it this time!"

Mean Old Mickle

There was once an old farmer who lived all alone in his little thatched cottage. His name was Mickle, and he was mean and selfish.

Mickle had a great deal of money. It was all in gold coins, and he was very fond of it. But he didn't tell anyone about the money – no, he kept it all to himself and didn't spend a penny if he could help it.

His cow gave him milk, his fields gave him corn for bread, his hens gave him eggs, and his sheep gave him wool for clothing. So Mickle grew rich, and each time he sold something for gold he put the gold piece into an old leather bag and hid it away.

He had a good hiding-place. The roof of his cottage was of thick straw thatch, and it was in the thatch that Mickle hid his bag of gold coins.

There was a very good place there, where the straw was thickest, about half-way between the eaves and the top of the roof, and there Mickle pushed his bag of money, drawing the straw over it so that no-one would guess a bag was hidden there.

Often people would ask Mickle for a little help. But always the mean old farmer shook his head.

"I'm poor," he said. "I've not enough for myself. I haven't a penny-piece to give away!"

Sometimes Old Mrs. Handy would come and ask for a shilling or two to help her over a bad time. She had often been good to Mickle, and cleaned out his cottage for him, but Mickle wouldn't help her.

"I'm a poor man," he said to her. "I've nothing to give you, unless you'd like to have two eggs out of the hen's nests for your breakfast."

But even that was not generous of him, for Mickle had already been round all the hen's nests and had taken the eggs for himself.

So Mrs. Hardy didn't find one, and she went without her breakfast.

Mickle liked his cows because they gave him milk, his sheep because they gave him wool, and his hens because they gave him eggs. He liked the pigs, too, but he did not like any other animals or birds.

He kept a dog because Rover barked at any stranger, but the poor dog was tied up all day long, and had hardly anything to eat. He kept a cat because she caught mice, but never did Mickle give the puss a drink of milk or a bite of bread.

As for the wild birds, Mickle hated them all. He threw stones at the sparrows, robbed any nest of young birds, and shouted at all the starlings that perched on his roof to preen their feathers after a bath in the pond.

It was the birds that punished Mickle for his meanness. This is how it happened.

One day a little wren flew down to the thatch of the roof to make a nest there. He pulled the straw this way and that with his beak, and he bit off the ends to make a hole.

And before he had gone very deep into the roof he came to the bag of gold that Mickle had hidden in the thatch!

The wren was an inquisitive little bird who liked to find out everything. The string of the bag was towards him, so he pecked at it. It undid like a long, black worm.

A little mouse ran up the thatch and spoke to the wren. "What have you found? Is it a worm?"

"Help me to pull," said the wren. "There is a bag hidden here. It might be full of food."

So they pulled at the string, but it was tied very tightly round the bag's neck and they could not undo it.

The little mouse had an idea. My teeth are sharp," he said. "I will gnaw at the bag, and then I may perhaps be able to make a hole and get at the food."

So he began to nibble at the bag. He nibbled and gnawed, and gnawed and nibbled, and at last he had made quite a big hole.

He put his nose into the bag and drew it out again. "There's no food there," he said "It's just something round and hard. Good-bye. I'm going to my hole!"

He ran off and left the wren alone. The little bird pecked a bright gold coin out of the bag and looked at it, head on one side.

"I know someone who would like that!" said the wren to himself. "The magpie would! That big black-and-white bird loves anything bright. I'll tell him, and maybe in return he will tell me if he finds any store of insects later in the year, when I have young ones to feed."

So the wren flew off to tell the magpie, who was most interested. The big bird flew back to the roof with the wren. But Mickle, the farmer, saw him and threw a stone at him. It struck the magpie on the tail and a feather fell out.

"I will come back again in the early morning before the farmer is awake!" called the magpie to the wren. So, the next morning, the magpie flew softly down and went to the hole in the thatch with the wren.

He put in his big beak and pulled out a bright coin. My goodness, wasn't he pleased!

"This is a lovely, shiny thing!" he cried, overjoyed. "Just what I love. I will take it to my nest. Are there any more?"

"Heaps!" said the wren, pleased that such a big bird should be so friendly to him. "Take what you want. They cannot be any use if they are left in the roof all the time."

So the magpie told his friends, and soon, in the very early morning, magpies, and jackdaws, too, came flying to get the shining things they loved. Soon there was not a single gold piece in the bag!

And, oh dear, what a shock for Mickle when he next took his bag down from its hiding-place in the roof! He couldn't believe his eyes.

"I've been robbed!" he yelled. "Yes, robbed! Every bit of gold is gone! Help! Police! Help!"

He tore down to the village, with tears streaming down his cheeks. He stopped everyone and told them.

"All my gold is gone! Eighty-seven pieces of it I had, well hidden in the roof! And now it is gone!"

But nobody would believe him. "You said you hadn't a penny-piece," said everyone.

"You said you were a poor man," said Mrs. Handy.

"You're making it up," said the policeman, and he wouldn't even go back to help Mickle look for the lost gold.

Well, it served him right! It is still in the nests of the magpies and the jackdaws, and one day, when those nests fall to pieces in the winter's rain and wind, the bright coins will fall down to the grass below – and, dear me, what a pleasant surprise all the children of the village are going to have!

I do hope you will find one, too!

Smack-Biff-Thud!

Mister Flick lived next door to Dame Tantrum. Flick was hot-tempered and Dame Tantrum was always flying into a rage, so very often there were shouts and yells coming from their gardens.

But for a long time there had been peace. Mister Flick was growing cucumbers in a frame to show at the Fruit and Flower Show in the village, and he was afraid of quarrelling with Dame Tantrum in case she threw rubbish into his garden and broke his frames.

Dame Tantrum was growing tomatoes out of doors, also for the Show, and she didn't want Mister Flick throwing rubbish into *her* garden either, in case it broke her beautiful tomato plants.

"Ha!" said Mister Flick to himself each morning, as he went to look at his long green cucumbers. "Ha! I'm quite sure there are no finer cucumbers in the village! I shall walk off with first prize, that's certain!"

And Dame Tantrum would look lovingly at her fat tomatoes getting red and round, and rub her hands together in delight. "Best tomatoes in the kingdom!" she said to herself. "And all grown in the open air too! I shall get first prize, there's no doubt of it!"

The great Fruit and Flower Show drew nearer. Mister Flick and Dame Tantrum grew excited. They looked at their cucumbers and tomatoes a dozen times a day. Mister Flick gave his cucumbers four canfuls of water each evening. Dame Tantrum gave her tomatoes a canful for each plant. And the green cucumbers and red tomatoes grew and grew and grew.

Now one evening Mister Flick cut a cucumber for his own supper. The same evening Dame Tantrum picked three ripe tomatoes for *her* supper, and they happened to see one another just going up the garden.

"Good evening," said Mister Flick. "Look at this cucumber. Did you ever see such a fine monster?"

"Good evening," said Dame Tantrum. "Look at my tomatoes! I'm sure you have never grown such beauties."

"I don't care for tomatoes," said Mister Flick. "Nasty soft things. Give me a cucumber any time!"

"I've never been able to understand what people see in cucumbers," said Dame Tantrum, offended. "No sweetness, all water and tough flesh!"

"Don't talk nonsense," said Mister Flick.

He held up his fine long curved cucumber and waggled it in front of Dame Tantrum's face. "Look at that for a fine cucumber!"

"Stop waggling the ugly thing under my nose!" cried Dame Tantrum, losing her temper. "It's a silly cucumber. Cucumbers sound silly and they look silly too!"

Mister Flick was angry. He shook the cucumber hard at Dame Tantrum, and, do you know, he shook it so hard that the top end flew off and hit Dame Tantrum on the nose!

Mister Flick was just as surprised as Dame Tantrum. When the old dame had got over her shock she screamed at Mister Flick. "You bad man! Throwing cucumbers at me! Well, I can do some throwing too. Take that!"

And she picked a nice ripe tomato out of her basket and threw it straight at Mister Flick. It hit him in the face, Splosh!

"Oh, oh, my beautiful cucumbers!" cried Mister Flick, looking at three that he had broken in half. "Oh, you bad-tempered old dame! Take my broken cucumbers!"

And Mister Flick began to throw the broken halves of his cucumbers over the wall at Dame Tantrum! Well, really! That was more than she could stand!

"I'm as good a shot as you!" she cried, and she threw her third tomato at Mister Flick. Plonk! It hit his forehead and the red juice dripped down Mister Flick's face. He quite lost his temper then.

"I'll teach you, I'll teach you!" he yelled, and he pulled at all the cucumbers he could see, waggled them hard at Dame Tantrum, and off flew the tops and hit her on the nose! Some people passing by stopped to gaze in surprise, and how they laughed!

Well, Dame Tantrum rushed to her tomato plants and pulled as many tomatoes as she could see. Soon she was pelting Mister Flick with them as if they were snowballs. Splash–thud–smack! And plop–biff! went the cucumbers! It was a sight to see!

"Ooooh!" said Mister Flick, astonished. "Now, Dame Tantrum, stop this! I won't have tomatoes thrown at me!"

"Oh, won't you! Well, have another!" said the cross dame, and she threw a second one at Mister Flick. He tried to dodge it and couldn't, and he fell back into one of his cucumber frames! By good luck the lid was off, so he didn't break any glass, but he sat down heavily on a fine cucumber plant!

Then Mister Plod the village policeman came by, and he was shocked. He went in at Dame Tantrum's garden gate and spoke sternly to the two sillies.

"Stop this at once!" he said. "Whatever do you think you are doing? I thought you were growing these lovely cucumbers and tomatoes for the Show!"

Mister Flick and Dame Tantrum stopped their throwing and stared at Mister Plod. Dame Tantrum suddenly saw dozens of beautiful tomatoes smashed on the ground, and Mister Flick saw his fine cucumbers all in bits!

"Oh, I shan't win any prize now!" they both wailed. And Dame Tantrum burst into tears, and Mister Flick went as red as one of the tomatoes!

"It serves you right," said Mister Plod sternly. "If you can't manage your tempers, you deserve to lose your prize vegetables. Clear up the mess, please."

They spent the evening clearing up the mess. It was dreadful to have to throw the cucumbers and tomatoes on the rubbish heap. Mister Flick saw Dame Tantrum crying, and felt sorry for her.

He poked his head over the wall. "I'm sorry about it all," he said. "Let's be friends. It's too late now to grow cucumbers and tomatoes for the Show this week, but we'll have supper together one night with a salad of young cucumbers and tomatoes!"

So they did – and now they are great friends. They mean to take the first prizes next year, whatever happens.

Chapter 3

Enid Blyton

The Strange Doll

Doreen was very sad. She had a lovely baby doll that could shut its eyes and could say "Mama" quite plainly – and now the doll was broken!

It wasn't really Doreen's fault. She had put it on the table in the kitchen just for a moment whilst she went to get her doll's pram – and Mummy hadn't seen it there. She had put down a tray of dirty cups and saucers, and the doll had fallen off the table.

Crash! Her pretty face broke into pieces, and both her legs broke, too. Doreen was very much upset and cried bitterly.

"Oh, Mummy, can't she be mended?" she asked. But Mummy shook her head. "No, I don't think so," she said. "She is too much broken. I'm afraid I can't buy you another doll just yet, darling, because I really haven't the money. You must wait for your birthday."

"But that's ever such a long time away," said poor Doreen. "Oh Mummy, I shan't have a doll to take out in my pram now!"

Doreen put the broken doll in the pram cupboard. Then she put her pram away – but when she took hold of the handle, she thought she would go down the lane to the farm and back again, even though she had no doll in the pram to wheel along. She would just pretend!

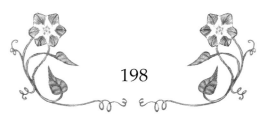

So off went the little girl, wheeling her empty pram. She went right down to the farm and then just turned to go back again.

Just as she turned, she heard a little whimpering noise. She looked round to see where it was. By the side of the lane, huddled under the hedge, was a puppy-dog. He was crying sadly all to himself.

Doreen went over to him. "What's the matter?" she asked. "Poor little puppy-dog, you are unhappy!"

The little dog whimpered again and did not move. "Come along!" said Doreen. "Come along! Don't sit under the damp hedge. Come out into the road and let me see you!"

But still the puppy did not move. So Doreen picked him up gently – and then she saw that he was hurt! One of his legs was bleeding, and he held it up as if it hurt him very much.

"Oh, dear!" said Doreen. "You're hurt! How did it happen? Did a farm-horse kick you – or a motor-car hurt you?"

The puppy whimpered again and licked Doreen on the face. He thought she was a dear, kind little girl. She put him down on the ground and tried to make him walk after her – but he was very much frightened, and would not move a step.

Doreen remembered that dogs have their names on their collars, so she took hold of his pretty red collar and looked at it. On it was printed: "White Cottage, Elmers End."

"Oh, you belong to Mrs. Harrison, who lives at Elmers End!" said Doreen. "Oh, dear – that's a long way away! I wonder if you can possibly get there."

The puppy yelped. He was trying to tell Doreen what had happened. His mistress had driven her car to the farm that morning and, just as she was leaving again, he had jumped out and hurt his leg. Now he was too frightened to do anything at all.

"However can I get you back?" said Doreen, patting the soft little head. "Oh! I've got such a good idea! I'll put you in my doll's pram, puppy! My doll broke this morning, poor thing, and the pram is empty. You'll fit in there nicely, because you are so small. I think I can manage to walk all the way to Mrs. Harrison's."

She picked up the puppy dog and put him gently into the doll's pram. He snuggled down on the pillow happily. It felt like his soft basket at home! Doreen pulled the covers over him and told him to go to sleep.

And so tired and frightened was the poor little puppy that he really did close his eyes and fall asleep in the pram! Doreen was so pleased.

"It's almost as good as having a doll!" she thought. Off she went, wheeling her pram carefully so as not to wake up the sleeping puppy-dog.

It was a long way to White Cottage where Mrs. Harrison lived. The little girl's legs were very tired long before she got there, but she didn't stop for a moment. She did so badly want to get the puppy back to his home and tell Mrs. Harrison to bathe his leg and wrap it up.

At last she came to White Cottage. Mrs. Harrison was in the garden, cutting roses. She looked up in surprise as she saw Doreen wheeling her pram up the path.

"Good morning, dear!" she called. "Have you come to show me your baby doll? What a long way you must have walked! You look quite tired!"

She went over to the pram and peeped inside – and how astonished she was to see a sleeping puppy there – her own puppy too! She stared and stared!

"Why, it's Sammy!" she said. "I thought I had left him behind at the farm and I was going to fetch him this afternoon!"

"I found him just near the farm, with a hurt leg," said Doreen. "I hadn't a doll in my pram to-day, because it got broken this morning. I was very sad about it because Mummy said it couldn't be mended, and she can't buy me another doll till my birthday. So I took my pram out empty – and it was a good thing I

did, really, because, you see, when I found poor Sammy, I could put him into the empty pram and wheel him all the way home to you. I think his leg wants bathing and bandaging, Mrs. Harrison."

What a to-do there was then! The puppy woke up and tried to jump out of the pram when it saw its mistress. Its leg hurt and it yelped. Mrs. Harrison called for warm water and an old handkerchief – and soon the little dog's leg was well

bathed and had a nice clean bandage on. He really looked quite proud of it.

"Well, now, my dear, it really is time for your dinner," said Mrs. Harrison, looking at the clock. "Good gracious! It's past one o'clock! Your mother will be worrying about you. I'll run you and your pram home in the car."

She took out her little brown car and popped the pram into the back seat. Doreen sat in the front and in a very little while they were back at Doreen's home. Mrs. Harrison explained to Doreen's mother how kind the little girl had been.

"She tells me her baby doll was broken this morning and that was how it came about that her pram was empty and she could take Sammy back to me," said Mrs. Harrison. "I was sorry to hear about her doll. Do give it to me, Mrs. White, for I am sure I can get it mended for her. I know a doll's hospital in the next town. I can get a nice new head and two new legs put on, I'm sure."

She took the doll away with her and – will you believe it – in three days she brought it back again, quite better! It had on a lovely new head, just as nice as the first one, and two beautiful fat legs. The doll smiled at Doreen, who hugged it and kissed it in delight.

"Oh, thank you, Mrs. Harrison!" she said. "You are kind!"

"Well, you were kind first!" said Mrs. Harrison, with a smile. "It's funny how things happen, isn't it? Your doll got broken – so you took your pram out empty – and found Sammy and put him into it – and I was pleased, and heard about your broken doll and wanted to get it mended for you! So your bit of kindness has come back to you and made you happy! I'm glad!"

But the gladdest person of all was Doreen, as you can guess!

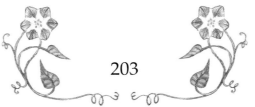

203

"Do Pass It On"

There was once a boy who liked doing kind things, and whenever people said to him – "It *is* kind of you to help me. Now what can I do for you in return?" – what do you think he said to them?

He said, "Oh, do pass it on! I don't want anything in return – just pass my bit of kindness on to somebody else. That's what my mother says we should do if people are good to us – pass it on!"

Well, that was a funny thing to say, but it was a very good idea. And now, just listen to what happened to a bit of kindness that was passed on!

Harry, the boy who began the bit of kindness, helped the old apple-woman to pick up the apples that fell out of her basket one morning. The old dame tripped over the kerb and down she went, with her apples all over the road! Dear, dear! She was so upset!

But along came Harry, helped her up, picked up all the apples, polished them with a clean handkerchief, and set them neatly back into the basket.

"You're a kind lad!" said the old apple-woman. "What can I do to repay you for your kindness? Will you have an apple?"

blew it over the hedge. It was almost in the mud. The apple-woman ran to it, and caught it before it got dirty. The washer-woman was so grateful. "That's kind of you," she said. "Very kind indeed."

"Do pass it on then!" said the apple-woman, pleased. "You pass on that bit of kindness, and don't forget!"

So the washer-woman thought about it and watched for a chance to pass it on. And very soon her chance came.

A little girl came down the road, crying. The washer-woman called out to her: "What's the matter, little girl?"

"No thank you," said Harry. "Just pass my bit of kindness on, will you?"

And off he went. "Very well!" thought the apple-woman. "I'll pass that bit of kindness on. I'll just wait and see how I can do it."

So down the road she went with her load, and very soon she came to where a woman was hanging out clothes on her line. Just as the apple-woman went by, the wind took hold of a pillow-case and

"Oh, I've been home, but my mother's out and I can't get any tea," wept the little girl. "And I'm so hungry!"

"Poor child!" said the washer-woman. "Come along in, and I'll give you some bread and treacle. I've got a bit of kindness to pass on to-day!"

So the child sat down and ate a great piece of bread and treacle. "You are very kind," she said shyly. "I wish I could give you back some bread and treacle."

"I don't want it, child," said the washerwoman. "Just pass the bit of kindness on – now don't forget. Do pass it on!"

The little girl ran off, pleased. She thought it was a funny idea to pass a bit of kindness on, but she made up her mind that she would. Her chance soon came. She passed a cottage where Mrs. Kelly lived with all her children, and saw poor Mrs. Kelly at the door, looking very worried. "What's the matter?" asked the little girl.

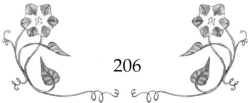

"Oh, I heard my Johnny's fallen down in the next street, and his leg's hurt so much he can't walk home," said Mrs. Kelly. "I want to go and fetch him, but I daren't leave the other children alone in the house – they're so little!"

"Well, I've got a bit of kindness to pass on," said the little girl. "I'll mind them for you, Mrs. Kelly!"

So Mrs. Kelly ran off to fetch Johnny, and the little girl minded the children and played with them. When Mrs. Kelly came back with Johnny, she was very grateful.

"I'd give you a penny for your kindness but I haven't one to spare," she said.

"Oh, I don't want any payment," said the little girl. "But, Mrs. Kelly, do pass it on!"

"Pass what on?" said Mrs. Kelly in great surprise.

"My bit of kindness!" said the little girl, laughing, and she ran home.

Well, Mrs. Kelly thought she certainly *would* pass it on, and she kept her eyes open to see how she could do it. She didn't have a wait very long.

When she passed the park gates with her children, she saw the park-keeper looking very miserable indeed.

"What's the matter, park-keeper?" she said. "Is your wife ill, or something?"

"Oh no," said the man. "But I forgot to bring my tea with me this afternoon, and I'm cold. I wish I had a drop of hot tea to warm me up!"

"Oh, I'll send my Bobby to fetch it for you," said Mrs Kelly at once. "He knows where your house is."

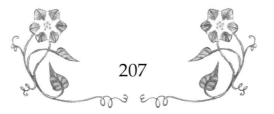

207

"What's up, Harry?" asked the keeper.

"My best ball's gone over the railings," said Harry. "I'm afraid someone else will find it in the morning. Then I shan't have it any more."

The keeper remembered the bit of kindness he had to pass on. "I'll go back to the park gates and unlock them for you," he said. "Then you can slip in and get your ball. What about that?"

"Thanks very much," said the park-keeper. "It's very, very kind of you. Anything I can do for you, by any chance?"

"No," said Mrs. Kelly. "Just pass it on, that's all!"

The park-keeper laughed. He promised he would, but he couldn't seem to think what to do. When six o'clock came, he rang the bell for everyone to go out of the park, and soon it was empty. He locked the gate behind him, and went on his way home, down by the park railings.

And just by the railings he saw a little boy looking upset. It was Harry, the one who began this story of passing on.

"Oh, I say, that is nice of you!" said Harry delighted. "But aren't you on your way home?"

"Oh, that doesn't matter," said the keeper. "I have got a bit of kindness to pass on, so perhaps this will do!" And back he went and unlocked the gates for Harry.

Harry got his ball and thanked the keeper. "Now just you pass that bit of kindness on!" said the keeper, smiling.

Well, wasn't it queer how Harry's own bit of kindness came back to him? He's busy passing it on again – and it may come to you this time. Do pass it on, won't you!

208

The Adventurous Ball

There was once a big round ball. It was all colours – red, yellow, blue, and green – and it looked very gay indeed when it bounced or rolled.

The other toys were rather impatient with the ball. They thought it a silly, dull creature. It could do nothing but bounce.

"What a life you lead!" said the sailing boat to the ball. "Nothing but bounce, bounce, bounce! Look at me! I go sailing on the river and on the pond. I even go on the sea at seaside time!"

"And what about *me*?" said the toy bus. "When I'm wound up I go round and round the nursery, and I carry dolls, bears, and rabbits for passengers! I have a fine life!"

"And I fly up in the air and see all kinds of things!" said the toy aeroplane.

"So do I!" said the kite. "I fly above the clouds and see the birds up there, and get as near to the sun as I can get!"

"And we dolls get about a lot too," said the curly-haired doll. "We go out in prams – we are taken out to tea – we do see the world! Poor, dull ball, you do nothing but bounce. We are sorry for you."

The ball felt sorry for himself, too. He had never felt dull before the toys had said all this to him, but now he really did feel as if he led a miserable sort of life.

However, the time came when all that was changed, as you will hear. It happened that the children in whose nursery the toys lived went off to the seaside for a holiday, and with them they took most of their toys. The bus went, the dolls went, the aeroplane, the kite – and the ball. What fun!

And then the ball's adventures began. It had longed and longed for adventures, and it was surprised when it had some. It had been taken down to the beach and left on the sand whilst the children dug castles. Nobody noticed that the tide had reached the ball. And no-one saw that it had taken away the ball when it began to go out again!

But it had! It bobbed the ball up and down on little waves, and took it right out to sea!

"Good gracious!" said the ball to itself. "I might be a little boat, the way I am floating along! Wherever am I going?"

A fish popped up its head and spoke to the ball. "Hello, big round fellow! What news of the land have you?"

The ball was proud to be able to tell news. It told the fish all about the other toys. Then the fish told the ball about the sea, and all the fishes and other sea creatures in it. "You are a bold, brave ball to go adventuring off by yourself like this," said the fish. "I do admire you!"

The ball bobbed on, prouder than ever. Soon a big white sea-gull swooped down and came to rest just by the ball. "Hello, big round fellow," he said in surprise. "I thought you might be food. How very bold of you to come adventuring on the sea like this!"

The ball felt proud – but it was a truthful ball. "Well, as a matter of fact, I can't very well help this adventure," he said. "The sea took me away."

"Tell me news of the land," said the gull. So the ball told all about the other toys, and the gull then told him of the gulls, and of their seaweed nests, and young brown gull-babies.

He told the ball of stormy days at sea. He showed him how he dived for fish. The ball was pleased and excited. How nice everyone was to him!

The ball bobbed in the pool and listened to the tales the crabs and shrimps told him He heard about the children who came shrimping with a big net. He saw how the little crabs could bury themselves in the sand in two twinks and not show even a leg. It was all very wonderful to the big ball.

When the tide went out again the ball went with it. It bobbed along merrily. Suddenly it saw a great big thing coming straight at it. Oh dear, oh dear – it was an enormous steamer! The ball felt sure it would be squashed to bits – but at the last moment it bobbed to one side and the big steamer sailed on. "Look! Look!" cried the people on the steamer, leaning over the side.

"There is a fine big ball, bobbing along all by itself!"

The ball was proud to be noticed by the people on the steamer. It bobbed after it for a long way but then got left behind. The tide took it once more and some great big waves curled over it and almost buried it. But it bobbed up gaily again; wondering what adventure it would have next.

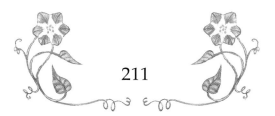

As it floated along it saw a little boat with two children in. "Look! Look! There's a beautiful big ball!" cried the boy. "Let's get it!"

The ball floated on. The tide turned again and flowed into a big bay. The ball floated by a boat and stayed there for a while. The boat spoke to him and told him how he sometimes went out fishing and how little boys and girls went rowing in him and used him for bathing. The ball had never known such a lot of things in his life. He would have stayed by the boat for a longer time, but a little wave came and took him away. He floated into a rock pool, and there the crabs and shrimps swam up to him in admiration.

"What a fine big round fellow you are!" they said. "Where do you come from? How brave of you to adventure all alone on the big, big sea!"

The boat was rowed after the ball. The boy leaned out and took it. He shook the water from it and showed it to his sister.

"Do you know, Winnie, I believe it is our very own ball – the one we lost yesterday!" said the boy. "See the colours on it! I am quite sure it is our own ball!"

"So it is!" said the girl. "I wonder where it has been all this time! I wish it could tell us its adventures. I expect it has had such a lot, bobbing up and down on the sea."

The children took
the ball back to shore. There
were all the other toys – the
aeroplane, the bus, the dolls, the kite,
and all the rest. How surprised they
were to see the ball again!

"We saw you floating away!" cried the
aeroplane. "Where did you go?"

"Ah," said the ball proudly. "I'm a big
round adventurous fellow, I am! I've
talked with birds and fishes, crabs and
shrimps – I've heard tales from boats –
I've nearly been run down by a great
steamer, and all the people on it saw me!
You may think I'm a dull fellow and can
do nothing but bounce – but you are
mistaken – I can float too – and I've had
more adventures than the whole lot of
you put together!"

And after that, as you can imagine,
none of the toys ever laughed at the ball
again for being a dull fellow who could
do nothing but bounce! He could tell
more stories than anyone else – and he
says he is going to float away again next
year and have some more adventures. I
wonder if he will!

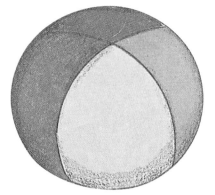

When Mrs. Tumpy Lost Her Head

Mrs. Tumpy lived in Peppermint Village in a little cottage called Toffee Roofs. She was a fat, round goblin woman, and all the elves, pixies and goblins in the village used to laugh at her because she fussed so much.

If one of her hens got loose she would run for miles asking anyone if they had seen it – and maybe it was under her henhouse all the while!

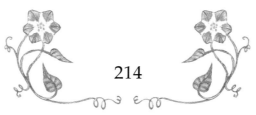

If she cut her little finger she would cry and scream, and somebody else would have to bind it up for her because she was so upset. And, dear me, one day when the wind caught her open umbrella and took her galloping down the village street, squealing for help, everyone thought she was being chased by robbers or something.

They came running out of their houses in fright. "Why, it's only that the wind has caught her open umbrella, like a ship's sail, and sent her scudding along," said Jinky, in disgust. "Hey, Mrs. Tumpy – leave go the handle and you'll be all right."

But Mrs. Tumpy was so scared that she quite lost her head. She wouldn't let go the umbrella handle, and the wind took her right to the duck-pond. She ran in at top speed and then sank. It took a long time to drag her out.

"Now, Mrs. Tumpy," said Jinky, when she was drying in front of his fire. "Listen to me. You fuss too much. You lose your head at the smallest upset. You are always making people think that something dreadful is happening to you, and all the time it's only a spider that has come out of a corner and made you jump – or something like that."

"Don't talk to me like that," said Mrs. Tumpy, crossly. "I won't have it."

"Well, you take my advice," said Jinky. "Don't lose your head too often – or one day it really will pop off and never come back!"

But Mrs. Tumpy took no notice of his words at all, and she still went on squealing at nothing, making terrible

fusses, and calling for help if she saw even an earwig.

So Jinky grinned a little grin to himself, and made up his mind to give Mrs. Tumpy a shock. He went to his grandmother, Dame Know-a-Lot, and asked her for a disappearing spell. She gave him one in a box. It was blue powder.

"Whatever it's blown on will disappear," said Dame Know-a-Lot, It will still be there, of course, but no-one will see it. Take care how you use it, Jinky."

Now that afternoon Jinky walked quietly by Mrs. Tumpy's garden. He peeped over the wall and saw what he had expected to see – Mrs. Tumpy fast asleep in a deckchair.

Jinky smiled to himself. He jumped over the wall, and went on tiptoe to Mrs. Tumpy. He took out his box of blue powder and blew it gently over her head. Then he went back over the wall.

He stood and watched. Mrs. Tumpy's head gradually faded away and disappeared. How peculiar she looked! Jinky could still hear her snoring. He tiptoed away, smiling.

Mrs. Tumpy soon woke up. She looked at her watch. Dear, dear, it was tea-time already. And Dame Quickly was coming to tea! Up she got and ran indoors. Soon she had the kettle on and went to the larder for the milk.

The cat had been there first. The jug was upset and the milk was on the floor. Mrs. Tumpy flew into a rage, and began to fuss around angrily.

"Oh dear, dear, dear! Now what shall I do? No milk, and there's Dame Quickly coming to tea. No time to get any more. Oh, where's that cat! Tabby, Tabby, Tabby!"

The cat came, but she didn't hear it. She turned to go to the stove and fell over it. Crash! She knocked her best teapot off the table.

"Oh, my, look at that! Nothing but bad luck today. Now what am I to do? Oh, goodness knows how I shall ever get the tea ready at this rate."

There was a voice outside the front door and Mrs. Tumpy heard the tap-tap-tap of Dame Quickly's stick as the old lady walked into the hall. "Now, now, Mrs. Tumpy, fussing again, and losing your head over something! Dear, dear."

Dame Quickly walked into the kitchen, and stopped in amazement, staring at Mrs. Tumpy.

"What's the matter?" said Mrs. Tumpy, crossly. "Haven't I done my hair?" She turned to look at herself in the big glass – and then she gave a scream of dismay.

"Where's my head? I've lost it! Oh, mercy me, what's happened to my head?"

"Oh, Mrs. Tumpy, we always said you'd lose it if you went on like that," said Dame Quickly, "and now you have."

"Oh, oh – what shall I do? Where's my head gone?" wept Mrs. Tumpy, and tears from where her head ought to be fell down the front of her dress. She looked all round the kitchen, but her head wasn't there. She even went and looked into the larder, but of course it was nowhere to be seen.

She ran out into the garden. "Has anyone seen my head?" she called to the astonished passers-by. "I've lost my head! Has anyone seen it?"
Now most people guessed at once that someone had put a spell on Mrs. Tumpy to make her head invisible, and they laughed. But they weren't going to tell Mrs. Tumpy why. Oh, dear me, no! Perhaps if she thought she really

had lost her head, she wouldn't make such silly fusses as she did.

So everyone shook their heads, and said the same thing. "No, Mrs. Tumpy – so sorry, but we haven't seen your head anywhere. Dear, dear, we always said you'd lose it if you went on kicking up such a fuss about everything."

Poor Mrs. Tumpy couldn't eat any tea, or any supper either. She spent all the evening looking in the most unlikely places for her lost head. She even looked in the coal-scuttle and under the bed.

She went to bed very unhappy indeed. "I can't clean my teeth or brush my hair because my head has gone," she groaned. And then she was so tired out that she fell asleep.

In the night the spell wore off. When she awoke and looked fearfully at herself in the glass, how excited she was to find that her head had come back again. She smiled and nodded at it. "So you're back. Welcome home to me! I *am* glad to see you. And I do promise I'll never lose you again, dear head, never, never, never!"

And she was very careful after that not to lose her head or fuss when anything went wrong. So Jinky's mischievous little spell did some good after all.

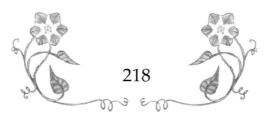

218

The House in the Tree

Eileen and Marigold lived next door to one another, and they played together every day. But they were quite different!

Eileen was lazy and wouldn't bother about anything. Marigold liked to work hard, and would help anyone she could. Eileen was eight and Marigold was seven. Eileen couldn't read and Marigold could. Eileen didn't even know her twice times table, but Marigold had already got as far as four times.

Eileen laughed at Marigold because she liked doing things. "You are silly to learn to read," she said. "Your mother won't read to you any more now."

"Oh yes, she will," said Marigold, "and I'll be able to read to myself, too, so I'll get twice as many stories!"

"Well, I can always get my mother to read to me whenever I want a story," said Eileen. "So what's the use of bothering to learn?"

"You are lazy," said Marigold. "You can't even knit, as I can – you can't even tie a bow!"

"Well, you couldn't last week!" said Eileen.

"But I can now," said Marigold. "Look – I tied my own shoe-laces this morning – one on each foot. It took me a long time, but I did it. Now I can tie them every morning."

"Pooh!" said Eileen, scornfully. "I can get my mother to tie mine in half the

time. What's the use of learning that if you've got someone to do it for you?"

Now one day, when Eileen and Marigold were playing in the wood, they heard the sound of someone squealing.

"Oooh! Oooh! Now look what I've done!"

Eileen and Marigold peeped round a tree to see who was squealing – and they saw a plump little woman sitting on a tree-trunk sucking her hand.

"What have you done?" asked Marigold.

"I was chopping wood for my fire when the chopper cut my thumb," said the little woman, her bright eyes twinkling at Marigold. "I shall have to bandage it."

"I'll do it for you," said Marigold. She took her clean hanky from her pocket and tore it into neat strips for a bandage. Then she quickly bound the little woman's thumb, and tied a neat little bow.

"What beautiful bows you tie," said the little woman, looking at her bandage. "Thank you very much. My goodness, my thumb does hurt. I don't believe I'll be able to dress my children for their party this afternoon!"

"Shall we help you?" asked Marigold.

"I don't want to," said Eileen, who was feeling lazy. "I want to play."

"Can you tie bows?" the little lady asked her, and Eileen shook her head. "Well, it's no use coming to help dress my children if you can't tie bows, because their party dresses have sashes – and they have to be tied in beautiful bows and each child has two plaits with bows at the end. So *you* wouldn't be any

help. But this little girl would be a great help. Come along in, my dear!"

"Where's your house?" asked Marigold, looking round.

"In here!" said the little woman, and she pressed a bit of bark on a great oak-tree. A round door swung open! Marigold stared in surprise. So did Eileen. The little woman went in at the door and pulled Marigold in too. The door shut with a bang.

There was such a dear little room inside the tree. It was quite round. There was a

table in the middle and a wooden seat ran all round. Seven small pixie children were sitting on the seat, as quiet as mice.

"Oh!" said Marigold, "Your children are fairies!" "Yes," said the little woman, and she shook out a pair of wings from under her shawl. "I'm a pixie too, but I usually cover up my wings in the wood in case anyone sees me. Now, children – get your dresses!"

Each child opened a tiny cupboard beneath the seat where she sat and pulled out gossamer dresses. They were in two colours – blue and yellow. The blue dresses had yellow sashes and the yellow dresses had blue sashes. Each child had two pieces of hair ribbon to match her sash. They all wore plaits and looked perfectly sweet.

What a busy time Marigold had! She tied seven sashes into beautiful bows! She tied fourteen hair-ribbons into fourteen bows on the ends of fourteen little plaits! The children were as good as gold. Their mother was so grateful to Marigold.

"I suppose you wouldn't take the children to their party for me, would you?" she asked. "My hurt thumb really makes me feel rather ill."

"Oh, I'd *love* to!" said Marigold at once. "Where is the party?"

"It is at the Princess Silvertoes' palace in the heart of the wood," said the little woman. "The children know the way. Tell the Princess about my thumb, won't you, and say I'm sorry I cannot come. Goodbye, dears!" They all went out of the tree. Eileen was still outside, wondering what had happened to Marigold. When she saw her coming out with seven beautifully dressed pixies she was most surprised.

"I'm taking these pixies to a party at Princess Silvertoes', in the heart of the wood," said Marigold to Eileen. "Go home and tell Mother I will be a bit late."

"I want to come too," said Eileen in excitement. "Well, you can't" said the pixies' mother, standing in the doorway. "You didn't want to help me at all. You can't even tie a bow! You are a lazy, good-for-nothing little girl, and I don't want you to go with my children. Go home!"

So whilst Marigold went to the party and had a wonderful time, poor Eileen had to go home in tears. And I shouldn't be surprised if she learnt to tie a bow the very next day! I hope *you* can tie a bow – you never know when it will come in useful, do you?

The Red-Spotted Handkerchief

R aggy the pixie had a red-spotted handkerchief that he was very proud of. It was a big one, with deep red spots all over it. Raggy always wore it in his front coat-pocket, where it stuck out a little so that everyone might see it.

Now one morning as Raggy was going along the road he wanted to sneeze. So he felt for his handkerchief to sneeze into – and it wasn't there!

Raggy was so surprised that he forgot to sneeze, which was a pity, for he really liked a good sneeze. He stood there feeling anxiously in all his pockets, but it wasn't in any of them.

"Somebody must have taken it!" said Raggy. "Yes – somebody at the meeting I've just been to! Oh how naughty of them! I'll go straight back and see who's got it! They will still be there talking."

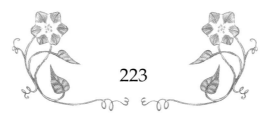

223

So back Raggy went and told everybody at the meeting that he had lost his red-spotted handkerchief.

"You lent it to Gobbo to wipe some spots off his coat," said Tag.

"But I gave it back!" said Gobbo at once.

"And you lent it to Hoppy to wave to his aunt when she passed by the window," said Tag.

"But I gave it back, I know I did!" said Hoppy. He turned out his pockets, and certainly there was no handkerchief there.

"And I lent it to *you*, Tag, to polish your silver watch-chain this morning!" said Raggy. "You must have kept it."

"Indeed I didn't!" said Tag. "I put it back into your pocket myself. Did you lend it to anybody else?"

"Yes, Raggy lent it to me to pop over my head when I went out in the sun to look for Jiggy," said Chuffle. "I tied a

knot in each corner – but I untied them when I came back, and gave the hanky back to Raggy. I know I did. It's no use looking at me like that, Raggy. *I* haven't got your handkerchief!"

"Well, it's a very funny thing," said Raggy, feeling angry. "I seem to have lent it to all of you this morning, and I haven't got it myself – so *one* of you must have kept it! It's very mean of you!"

"Very well, Raggy, we'll all turn out our pockets and *show* you that we haven't got it!" said Hoppy. And everyone turned out his pockets for Raggy to see. There were sweets and tops and string and money – but no red-spotted handkerchief.

"Now you turn out *your* pockets, Raggy!" said Hoppy. "We'll make quite sure you're not making all this fuss for nothing!"

So Raggy turned out his pockets, but there was no handkerchief there either.

"It's not a bit of use," said Raggy! "*One* of you has my

beautiful handkerchief, and it's very wrong of you!"

"Now, Raggy, when you left the meeting, I *know* I saw your red handkerchief sticking out of your front coat-pocket," said Chuffle. "I just know I did. So if you took it away yourself, we couldn't have kept it! Did you meet anyone on your way home?"

"Well, go on," said Hoppy.

"And after a bit I saw a cow looking over a hedge," said Raggy.

"Did you lend *her* your handkerchief?" asked Chuffle.

"Really, Chuffle, do you suppose I go about lending cows my handkerchief?" said Raggy! "I suppose you think she wanted to polish her shoes with it? Well, she didn't!"

"Go on. What did you do next?" asked Hoppy.

"Well, let me see," said Raggy. "Oh, I know – a car came suddenly round the corner, and I had to jump quickly into the hedge – and I fell over and hurt my knee very badly."

"Did you really! Poor old Raggy," said Hoppy, for he knew how painful it was to fall down. "Did your knee bleed?"

"Oh, terribly!" said Raggy. "I had to bandage it…"

He suddenly stopped and went very red indeed. He didn't finish what he was going to say.

"Go on," said Tag.

"No, nobody!" said Raggy.

"Tell us exactly what you did," said Hoppy.

"Well," said Raggy, "I left the meeting, and walked up the road. I met a dog with a black head,"

"Did you lend *him* your handkerchief?" asked Tag.

"No, of course not," said Raggy. "What would a dog want a handkerchief for? To wave to the engine-driver of the train, or something? Don't be silly."

226

"Oh, that's all," said Raggy. "Well, I don't think I'll bother any more about my handkerchief. Good-bye, everyone."

"No, no, Raggy, don't go yet!" said Tag, and he held him by the arm. "Let's see your poor hurt knee!"

"Oh, it's quite all right now," said Raggy.

"It might not be," said Tag. "We'd better look and see if it wants bathing. Turn up your trouser leg, Raggy."

So Raggy had to, and his knee was neatly bound up with – what do you think? Yes – his red-spotted handkerchief!

"I don't wonder you feel ashamed of yourself," said Tag sternly. "Coming back here and making all that fuss, when if only you'd thought for a moment you'd have known quite well where your silly old handkerchief was all the time!"

"I'm sorry," said Raggy, and he went home feeling very much ashamed. He didn't like to wear his handkerchief any more, so now it is neatly folded in his drawer. Silly old Raggy – he did make a mistake, didn't he?

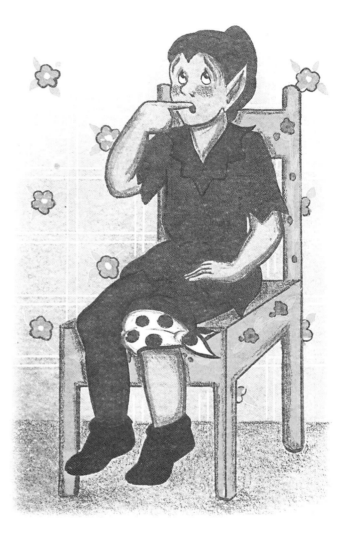

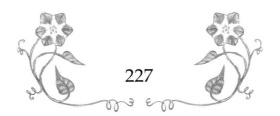

The Little Toy Stove

Angela had a little toy stove. It was a dear little stove, with an oven that had two doors, and three rings at the top to put kettles or saucepans on. At the back was a shelf to warm plates or keep the dinner hot. Angela liked it very much.

But Mother wouldn't let her cook anything on her stove. "No, Angela," she said, "you are not big enough. I am afraid you would burn yourself if you lighted the stove and tried to cook something."

"Oh, but Mother, it isn't any fun unless I can cook myself something!" said Angela, nearly crying. But Mother wouldn't let her light the stove, so it was no use saying any more.

Now one day, as Angela was playing with her saucepans and kettles in the garden, filling them with bits of grass for vegetables, and little berries for potatoes and apples, pretending to cook them all for dinner, she heard a tiny voice calling to her.

"Angela! Angela! Do you think you would mind lending me your stove for this evening? My stove has gone wrong, and I have a party. I simply *must* cook for my guests, and so I wondered if you'd lend me *your* stove!"

Angela looked all round to see who was speaking. At last she saw a tiny elf, not more than six inches high, peeping at her from behind a flower.

"Oh!" said Angela in delight. "I've never seen a fairy before. Do come and let me look at you."

The elf ran out from behind the flower. She was dressed in blue and silver, and had long shining wings and a tiny pointed face. Angela thought she was lovely.

"Will you lend me your stove?" asked the elf. "Please say yes."

"Of course!" said Angela. "I'd love to. Will you really cook on it? My mother won't let me."

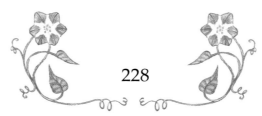

"Of course she won't let you," said the elf. "You aren't big enough yet. You might burn yourself."

"Shall I leave my stove here for you?" asked Angela.

"Yes, please," said the elf. "I can easily cook out here. It is to be an open-air party. I live behind those hollyhocks, so I shan't have far to bring my things."

"I suppose I couldn't come and watch you?" said Angela longingly. "I've never seen my toy stove really doing cooking, you know!"

"Well, you come and watch to-night," said the elf. "I shall begin my cooking at nine o'clock. The party begins at eleven."

Angela was so excited when she went in to bed. She meant to put on her dressing-gown and get up at nine o'clock, and creep down the garden.

So she lay awake until she heard the hall clock chime nine. Then up she got and slipped down the stairs and out of the garden door.

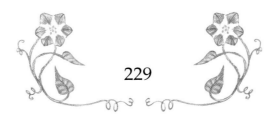

She could quite well see where her toy stove was, because smoke was rising from it. The elf had got it going well. A lovely smell of baking and roasting came on the air. Oooh!

You should have seen the elf cooking on that stove. The oven was full of things roasting away well. The plates were getting nice and hot in the plate-rack!

"Just listen to my pudding boiling away in that saucepan," said the elf, pleased. "This stove cooks very well indeed; it's a fine stove."

"What sort of pudding is it?" asked Angela.

"It's a tippy-top pudding," said the elf. "And I'm cooking a poppity cake too and some google buns."

"Oh my, they do sound delicious," said Angela, "and so exciting! I've never heard of them before. I suppose I couldn't come to the party?"

"No," said the elf. "It is too late a party for little girls like you. But, Angela, as I think it is really very kind of you to let

me use your lovely stove for my cooking, I'd like you to taste some of my dishes. Listen! There is sure to be some tippy-top pudding, some poppity cake, and a few google buns over after the party. If there are I will put them on a plate and leave them inside the oven. See? I will clean the stove nicely, too, and leave it all shiny and bright. Now, good night, dear. You must go to bed. You are yawning."

"Good night!" said Angela, and she ran off. In the morning she went to see if there *was* anything inside her oven. And what do you think? There was a neat little blue dish, and on one side of it was a slice of yellow tippy-top pudding, and on the other side were three google buns, red and blue, and a large slice of green poppity cake! Ooooh!

Angela ate them all – and they were simply delicious. She *does* so hope the elf will want to borrow her stove again. Wouldn't it be lovely if she did?

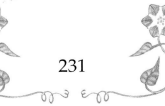

The Proud Little Pig

There was once a little pig who was very proud. He lived with his brothers and sisters in a sty in a farmyard, but he didn't like them at all.

"You are all so *stupid*," he said to his family. "Why, you can't even say 'Boo!' to the old goose who comes and looks at us through the gate."

"Why *should* we say 'Boo'? asked his mother, who was large and fat and round.

"Because that is what people always do say to a goose," said the little pig. "I'm surprised you don't know that."

"Don't be cheeky," said his mother, and she poked him with her big snout so that he rolled over in the mud. He was very angry.

"I don't like belonging to this family," he said in a grunty voice, turning up his nose at everyone. "What do you do all day long? Eat and gobble, gobble and eat! Greedy fat creatures!"

"Well, really, Piglet, you shan't talk like that!" said his mother, and she caught hold of his very curly tail and bit it hard. How the piglet squealed! He tore round and round the sty, trying to lick his tail, but he was so round and fat that he couldn't bend far enough.

"I shall not live with you any more!" he said to his family, who stood grunting with laughter at him. "I shall pack my bag and go and live with someone who is far wiser and cleverer than any of you. I am wasted here! Good-bye!"

And off he went, taking his little bag with him, with his toothbrush, sponge, and winter scarf inside.

"Where are you going?" grunted his mother.

"I shan't tell you!" said the pig. And indeed, he *couldn't* tell her, because he didn't know himself.

As he trotted along, carrying his bag in his mouth, he thought hard. "I must think of a good clever name for myself," he said. "Piglet is a stupid name. I will call myself Mr Grunt. That sounds grand."

So Mister Grunt scampered on and on and at last he came to a wood. He crept under a bush to rest, and there he found a hole leading deep underground. He sniffed down the hole and knew that someone lived there. So he called down:

"Who lives here?"

"Mister Reynard the Fox," came the answer.

"Who's that at my front door?"

"Mister Grunt," said the piglet in a haughty sort of voice. "Are you a clever person, Mister Reynard? I have left my family and am looking for a really wise person to live with."

The fox grinned. He knew quite well that Mister Grunt was a pig, for he could smell him.

"You are nice and fat," said the fox.

"I am very wise," said the pig.

"You are the plumpest pig I have ever seen," said the fox.

"I have left my family because they were so stupid," said the pig.

"I am simply *longing* for my dinner," said the fox, and he looked at the pig in such a queer way that he was quite alarmed.

"Come along in, Mister Grunt," called the fox. "I'm sharp enough, as anyone will tell you – and I'd like someone smart to live with me and keep me company."

So down the hole trotted the pig, with his little bag. He didn't much like the smell, because it was even stronger than his own pigsty. He bowed to Mister Reynard, who licked his lips when he saw the fat little pig.

"How do you do?" asked the pig. "I am a clever pig."

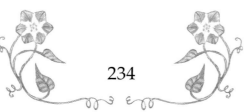

path went up it, so the pig went up it too. He was soon panting and puffing, and his bag seemed very heavy. He made the curl in his tail as stiff as he could, and hung the bag on that. It was so difficult to pant and puff with a bag in his mouth.

Now, at the top of the mountain, hidden away in the rocks, was the nest of two big eagles. They had young ones in the nest, and they fed them every day with rabbits, small birds, and other creatures.

The pig came to the nest, and stopped in surprise when he saw two big eagles sitting quietly there, their hooked beaks turned towards him, and their sharp eyes gleaming.

"Good morning," said the pig. "I am Mister Grunt, a very wise pig. Are you clever too?"

"Very," said one eagle "Of course," said the other.

"Well, perhaps you would like me to live with you then," said the piglet eagerly. "I have left my stupid family, and I am looking for a new home with wise folk."

"You are very fat, Piglet," said the first eagle. "As plump as can be, Piglet," said the other.

And then he heard a rabbit's voice calling down the hole warningly:

"People who go down this hole don't come back! Beware!"

Well, that was quite enough for the pig. Before the fox could grab him, he scuttled backwards up the hole and rolled over on the bracken outside. In a trice he was away, scampering through the wood. The fox didn't go after him, for he disliked hunting in the sunlight. It hurt his eyes.

The pig ran for a long way. At last he came to a very steep hill. It was a mountain, but he didn't know it. The

"My name is Mister Grunt," said the pig in rather a haughty way.

"You are deliciously round," said the first eagle, and his beak snapped open and shut.

"You would make the finest dinner in the world, Piglet," said the second eagle dreamily. "Come nearer."

The little pig was alarmed. Good gracious. Here was someone else wanting to eat him!

He galloped over the top of the mountain with his bag, caught his foot in a root, and rolled over and over and over and over till he came to the very bottom at the other side!

Goodness! He had no breath left, and he felt bruised all over. He lay where he was for a moment, and then, seeing two big specks flying in the sky, he got up quickly. He was sure the two specks were

the eagles looking for him! He hurried away as fast as he could.

"It's too bad," he thought. "Too bad! Why must all the clever people I meet want to eat me? They seem to think more of my body than of my brains. It's too bad!"

Now at last he came to a house, built by a running stream. It looked a nice cosy house, and smoke came from the chimney. There was a sound of talk and laughter inside, and the little pig felt that here, perhaps, he could make his home.

So he knocked timidly on the door.

"Come in!" cried half a dozen voices. He went in. He saw a family sitting round the table – a mother and father and four children, all merry and bright eyed.

"Good-day," said the pig. "I am Mister Grunt. I have left my stupid family and I would like to live with a clever one. You look very clever to me."

"Oh, we are, we are!" they all cried. "Shut the door Mister Grunt and come along in."

"I have a lot of brains," said the pig, pleased to be welcomed like this. "I would make good company for you."

"We are sure of it!" cried the family. "You look very wise and smart."

The pig was really delighted. His tail curled more tightly than ever, and his snout lifted high in the air.

"I will live with you," he said. "May I join your meal? I am very hungry, for it is a long time since I left my sty."

"Of course!" said the father, and he set a chair for the pig. We have a lovely dinner to-day. We are eating a dish of sausages."

SAUSAGES! SAUSAGES! The little pig looked at the family in horror! Hadn't he heard his mother say that naughty pigs were made into sausages?

Oh dear, oh dear, oh dear! This was worse than anything he had heard that morning!

Picking up his bag he fled out of the door, as fast as ever he could, not even stopping to shut it. Sobbing and crying the proud little pig trotted along, trying to get as far from the house as he could. If only he had never left his nice, comfortable, safe pigsty!

He wandered on for miles, and suddenly he heard the sound he knew. It was Rover, the old farm-dog, barking!

The little pig had found his way home again, and there he was, outside his farmyard! He trotted in and went to the sty.

"Mother!" he yelled. "I've come back again."

"Snouts and tails!" said his big mother in surprise. "I thought you were too clever to live with us!"

"Oh, Mother. I made a mistake," said the pig. "I was very stupid to go out into the big world, for there everyone wants to eat me. But here I am safe, and I think it is better for a pig to be stupid and safe than clever and eaten!"

"Come under the gate then," said his Mother. "And don't let us hear any more about being clever."

So under the gate he went, and never once did he grumble again at his family. But do you know, he had such a fright that all the curl come out of his tail. So if you go to a pigsty you'll know which is Mister Grunt, won't you? – the pig with the very straight tail!

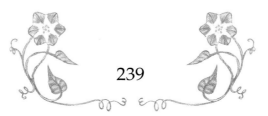

The Pantomime Cat

"**M**ollie! John!" called Mummy. "Where are you? I want you for a minute."

The two children were playing out in the garden. They ran in.

"I hear that old Mrs. Jones isn't well," said Mummy. "She can't go out and do her shopping. Now I think it would be very nice if you two children did her errands for her each day until she is better."

"Oh, Mummy, I don't like Mrs. Jones!" said Mollie. "She always looks so cross!"

"And she never gives anyone a penny, or a biscuit, or a sweet, or anything," said John.

"You don't do kind things for the sake of pennies or sweets," said Mummy. "You know that. You do it because it is good to be kind. You like me to be kind to you?"

"Yes," said Mollie. "We love you for it, Mummy! All right. We'll go – won't we, John!"

They were good-hearted children, so each day at ten o'clock in the morning they ran up the hill to Mrs. Jones's little cottage, knocked on the door and asked her what errands she wanted running.

Mrs. Jones never seemed very pleased to see them, and certainly she never gave them anything, not even a sweet out of her peppermint tin. She was not a very kind old lady and, although the children were polite to her, and always ran her errands cheerfully, they thought she was a cross old thing, and were glad when they had finished going to the grocer's, the baker's and the fishmonger's each day.

It was the Christmas holidays, and circuses and pantomimes were in every big town. There was a pantomime in the town where Mollie and John lived too, and children often stopped outside the big theatre and looked at the pictures.

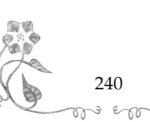

It's Dick Whittington and his Cat," said Mollie. "Last year it was Aladdin and the Lamp. I do wish Mummy would take us John."

But Mummy had said no, she hadn't enough money for all of them. Perhaps they would go next year.

"You said that last year Mummy," sighed Mollie. "I do wish we were rich! I'd love to go every night and see Dick Whittington and his clever cat. A girl I know has been, and she says the cat is ever so big and so funny that she laughed till she couldn't laugh any more!"

"Now it's ten o'clock," said Mummy. "Off you go to Mrs. Jones. You won't have to do her errands much longer because she can walk quite well now. You have been good children to run them so cheerfully."

Off went Mollie and John up the hill. They knocked at Mrs. Jones's door and went in. She was sitting at the table, sewing something with a big needle.

The children looked at it. It was a strange thing she was sewing – like a big, black fur rug – with a cat's head. "Whatever is that?" asked Mollie, in surprise.

"Always asking questions!" grumbled the disagreeable old woman. "It's the cat skin my son wears in the pantomime. Didn't you know he was the Cat in Dick Whittington this year?"

241

"Oh, no!" cried both children in delight. "How perfectly lovely!"

"Hmmm!" said Mrs. Jones, snapping off her thread. "Not so very lovely, I should think – nasty hot thing to wear every night for hours on end. Hmmm! Now listen – my son wants this cat costume this morning before eleven, so pop down now straightaway and say you've brought his costume. That's all I want you to do to-day. After this morning I can do my own shopping, so I won't be seeing you any more."

She wrapped up the parcel and the children sped off. "Mean old thing!" said Mollie. "Never even said thank you to us! I say! What fun to be going in at the stage door of the theatre! We might see some fairies – you know – the ones that sing and dance in the pantomime!"

They soon arrived at the stage door and asked the old man there for Mr. Jones.

"Go up the stairs and knock on the second door on the right," said the old

chap. Mollie and John ran up the stone steps and knocked on the second door.

"Come in!" shouted someone – and in they went.

A round, jolly-faced man was sitting in front of the mirror. He smiled when he saw them. "Hallo!" he said. "Have you brought my cat skin? Thanks awfully! I say are you the two children who have been running errands for my mother all this time?"

"No, we haven't," said John. "Mummy can't afford to take us this year – but, oh, you must look lovely! I wish we could see you!"

"Well, you shall!" said the jolly man, unwrapping the parcel. "You shall have free tickets every night of the week, bless your kind little hearts! That's your reward for being kind to someone who never said a word of thanks! I've some free tickets to give away – and my mother never wants to use them – so you shall have them! Would you like that?"

"Oh, yes!" shouted the children, their faces red with delight. "Yes, yes, yes! We shall see Dick Whittington – and the fairies – and you – and everything else! Oh, what luck!"

Well, it all came true – they did see the pantomime, every night of the week! The jolly man gave them their tickets and, oh, how they loved every minute of it!

"Yes," said Mollie shyly.

"And I guess she never said thank you did she? Or gave you a penny between you," laughed the man. "She's a funny old thing, but she means well. Have you seen me in the pantomime, dressed up in this cat skin?"

"The cat is the best and funniest of all!" said Mollie and John. "We do love him! And we are proud of knowing him, Mummy! Fancy knowing the pantomime cat! All the other boys and girls wish they were us!"

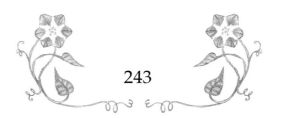

"Ah! You didn't know you were running errands for the pantomime cat's mother, did you?" said Mummy. "You never know what will happen when you do a kindness!"

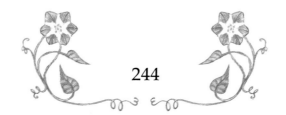

The Goblin Who Stole Sweets

Somebody was stealing sweets out of the toy sweet-shop in the nursery! There were twelve bottles of sweets there – and every day some of them disappeared.

"*I'm* not stealing them!" said Teddy bear.

"And I wouldn't touch *one*," said the toy soldier, though he was very fond of sweets.

"Well, someone's stealing them," said the Dutch doll. "And what Janet and Ronnie will say when they find out that their toy-shop sweets are gone, I really can't think!"

"We must find out who is taking them," said the blue rabbit. "They disappear in the afternoons, when the children are out for their walk and we are shut up in the toy-cupboard."

"Well, this afternoon we will take the key of the cupboard away, so that Nanny can't lock the door!" said Teddy. "Then we'll creep out and see who is the thief."

So that afternoon, when Janet and Ronnie had gone out for a walk, and had left the toys in the cupboard, they all crept out and hid in different places in the nursery, so that they might watch for the robber.

245

The toy soldier sat up on the nursery window-sill behind the curtain. He looked out of the window.

"Ooooh!" he said. "It's snowing! There is a white carpet all over the ground. I can see all the way down the hill, and there's snow everywhere. I wish we could toboggan!"

"Sh!" said the blue rabbit. "Somebody is coming!"

And sure enough somebody was! It was a little green goblin, with a long nose and ears, and naughty eyes. He slipped in at the door, and ran to the toy sweet-shop. In a trice he picked up two of the bottles of sweets, and was just going to uncork them when the toy soldier shouted at him:

"Stop, thief! You naughty robber! Put down those bottles at once!"

The goblin jumped. He looked round – but when he only saw toys watching him, he grinned.

"Shan't!" he said.

"You jolly well will!" said the teddy, and he rushed at the goblin. But quick as lightning the little green fellow ran to the door and out. He slipped into the garden and ran to the gate. Then,

staggering about in the thick snow, he began to go down the white hillside with the two bottles of sweets.

"He's taken two whole bottles!" said Teddy.

"Stop him!" said the blue rabbit.

"How?" asked the Dutch doll, very worried.

Come on, I'll show you!" yelled the toy soldier suddenly, and with one leap he was down from the window-sill. He caught up the tin nursery tray and rushed outside, followed by all the rest of the toys. They ran to the gate quite easily, for the snow had been swept away from the path.

"But how can we get down this snowy hill?" asked the Dutch doll, in dismay.

"That's what I brought the tray for – to get down the hill before the goblin does!" cried the toy soldier, and he slammed the tray on the snow at the top of the hill. "Get on, everyone."

They all got on, though the blue rabbit was very much afraid. The toy soldier gave the tin tray a push and leapt on at the back. The tray slid down the hill.

Whoooooooosh! What a slide it was! The tray sped on over the snow like a toboggan, and carried all the toys with it. My word, what a pace it went! You should have seen it! The blue rabbit's whiskers were almost blown off.

The green goblin was still staggering down the hill, deep in the snow. The tray sped after him.

"Whoooooooosh!" cried all the toys. "Look out!"

The goblin heard the noise and looked behind him. He gave a yell. The tray was almost on top of him. He tried to jump out of the way, but it wasn't any good.

Bang! The tray hit him in the back and sent him deep into the snow. He disappeared into the whiteness, and all the toys fell off the tray.

"Ooooh!" said the toy soldier.

"I've bent my whiskers," said the blue rabbit.

"Where are those bottles of sweets?" cried the bear. "Oh – here's one."

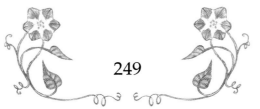

"And here's another!" shouted the Dutch doll, picking the second one up from the snow."

"But where's the goblin?" asked the toy soldier.

"We'd better dig him out," said the rabbit.

"Look! There are the children coming home from their walk!" cried the teddy. "We must get home quickly before they see us. Never mind the goblin!"

They all scrambled back up the hill, and in at the nursery door. They shook the snow off themselves as best they could, stood the tray in the corner, and scurried into the cupboard – only just in time!

"I can't think why our toys feel so wet," said Janet, when she opened the cupboard and took them out. "I'd very much like to know what they've been doing!"

Well, if she asked the green goblin, she'd soon know what the toys had been up to. But, dear me, the green goblin was at the bottom of the snow! And there I'm afraid he'll have to stay till it melts. Serves him right, the naughty little thing!

Big-Eyes the Enchanter

Big-Eyes the Enchanter had found a most marvellous spell. It was made of moonshine, starlight, the roots of mountains, the footfalls of a weasel, the breath of a fish and the smell of rain. It was stirred up with a Hoodle-Bird's tail-feather and boiled on a piece of shining ice.

It was the most powerful spell in the world. It would make Big-Eyes the Enchanter King of all the Lands on Earth. He could do what he liked. Ah, what a time he would have!

Big-Eyes was not a pleasant fellow. He didn't like flowers, he didn't like animals, he hated children. He couldn't bear fairies, he spanked every elf he met, and he hated to hear anyone laughing.

"When I use my spell and make myself King of all the Lands on Earth, I will destroy the flowers everywhere!" he cried. "I will shut all the animals up underground, and I will make all the boys and girls work hard for me from the moment they are three years old. As for the fairies and the elves, the goblins and the pixies, I'll send the whole lot to the bottom of the sea. Ho, what a time I'll have!"

He looked at the spell. It was shimmering in a great blue cauldron, stirred by his servant, a big lad with a stupid, grinning face.

Then Big-Eyes looked at his book of magic. He wanted to find out exactly when the spell would work. At last he found what he wanted to know.

"This spell when made will only act on Midsummer Day at five o'clock in the morning," he read. "Aha! Then I'll set my alarm clock for half-past four, and get the spell working at five exactly. Then thunder and lightning will come and when the spell has stopped everyone will be my slave."

The night before Midsummer Day the Enchanter set his alarm clock to go off at half-past four. Then he went to bed, full of excitement to think of all the power that would be his next day. His servant, the grinning lad, had been told to keep awake all night, and stir the spell to keep it sweet.

The Enchanter had exciting dreams. He dreamt that he was a monarch on a golden throne, set with all the rare jewels of the world. He dreamt that not a single flower blossomed on the earth. He dreamt that all the puppies and kittens, chicks and ducklings, calves and lambs were hidden away from the sunshine deep in the heart of the earth. He dreamt that all the boys and girls no longer played but worked all day long for him.

Sweet dreams for the wicked Enchanter! On he dreamt and on – and at last woke up. No alarm bell woke him – he woke up himself. He looked at

the clock. It was half past three. Not time to get up yet. He lay and waited. Then he looked at the clock again, when about half an hour had gone.

It was still half-past three. What a strange thing! The Enchanter listened for a moment – and he could hear no ticking! The clock had stopped at half-past three in the morning. He had forgotten to wind it up in his excitement the night before!

The village clock began to strike outside. One – two – three – four – five – six! Six o'clock! The right minute for the working of the spell was past! It wouldn't come again until a year was past!

In a fearful rage the Enchanter sprang out of bed. Why hadn't the servant lad warned him, when the clock had stopped? He was supposed to keep awake all night and stir the blue cauldron!

The boy was fast asleep, poor lad, his head resting on the cauldron. Big-Eyes took him by the shoulder and shook him in fury. The boy woke up in fright, and, thinking that the Enchanter was a thief come in the night, he struck out with all his might.

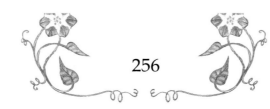

Biff! The Enchanter fell to the ground, and as he fell he caught at the cauldron to save himself. Sizzle-sizzle-sizzle! The shimmering spell inside upset all over him as he lay on the ground.

The servant lad watched in terror. What would his master do to him now? He would beat him, surely, or at least turn him into a frog or beetle.

The spell acted strangely. It altered the Enchanter bit by bit. He changed slowly into an old man – an old ragged man with a long ragged beard and bald head. He became a beggar-man, and slowly rose from the ground and went to stand at a corner to beg from the passers-by. And little children were sorry for him and gave him pennies.

Sometimes he remembered how he had been the great Enchanter, and then he would shake his head and mutter: "Ah! I could have ruled the world! But I forgot to wind up the clock!"

As for the servant lad, what became of him? He got such a terrible fright that he ran off to sea, and one day he told his story to me. At the end he shook his head and said: "Ah, it was a good thing my master forgot to wind up his clock that night!"

And dear me, I think it was too!

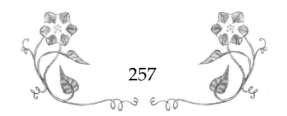

The Kickaway Shoes

Skip and Jump were very busy brownies. They had been spring-cleaning their cottage from top to bottom – and my, what a lot of rubbish they had turned out!

"Look at that!" said Skip, pointing to an enormous pile of old kettles, old books, and old boots and shoes he had put in their back garden. "Whatever are we going to do with all this rubbish?"

"And look at my pile of rubbish, too!" said Jump. Skip looked. It certainly was an even bigger pile than his. There was a broken-down iron bedstead, two chipped vases, an old enamel candlestick, four saucepans with holes in – oh, and heaps more things.

"What are we going to do with them?" asked Skip. "We can't burn them, they won't burn."

"And we haven't got a dustman in our village," said Jump. "So we can't ask him to collect our rubbish."

"And we are *not* going to throw these old things into the ditches, as lots of untidy people do," said Skip. "That would spoil the countryside. So what *are* we to do?"

"I say – what about borrowing those Kickaway Shoes belonging to old Grumpy Gnome!" cried Jump, all at once. "They would soon take our rubbish away!"

"Ooh, yes," said Skip. "But I'm afraid of the Grumpy Gnome. He's so bad-tempered, and I don't trust him."

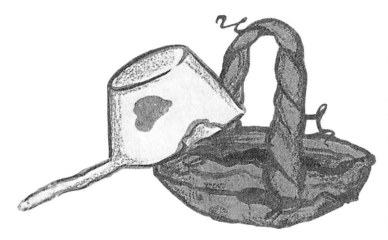

"Well, if we pay him for the loan of his magic shoes, he can't be angry with us," said Jump. "Just think, Skip! Whatever we kick with the Kickaway Shoes immediately disappears! It's wonderful! If I kicked that old saucepan there with a Kickaway Shoe, it would fly away and we'd never see it again! Ooh, it wouldn't take us long to get rid of all our rubbish then, would it?"

"And what fun it would be to do some magic kicking!" cried Skip, jumping

about in excitement. "What fun! Let's go and ask Grumpy Gnome now."

"We'll take a piece of gold with us," said Jump, running to his purse, which was on the mantelpiece. "He is sure to charge us a lot. He is a greedy, selfish, horrid fellow, and nobody likes him. We won't stay long, in case he puts a nasty spell on us."

Off went the two brownies in great excitement. Jump had the piece of gold safely in his pocket. They soon came to Grumpy's cottage. It was built into the hill-side, and there was a red door with a big black knocker. Jump knocked loudly. Rat-tat-tat!

The Grumpy Gnome opened the door and glared at them. He was a nasty-looking person. He had yellow whiskers and a very long nose. His eyes were small and he wore on his head a round red cap with little silver bells all round the rim. They rang when he walked. It was a magic cap, and he never took it off, not even to brush his hair. So nobody knew whether he had any hair or not.

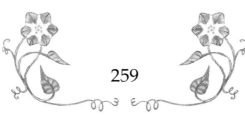

"What do you want?" he said, in his loud deep voice.

"Please would you lend us your Kickaway Shoes?" asked Jump politely. "We will pay you for the loan of them."

"I shall want a piece of gold," said the Grumpy Gnome, nodding his head till all the silver bells on his cap rang loudly.

"We have brought you a piece," said Jump, and he showed the gold to Grumpy. The gnome's little eyes shone at the sight of the gold, and he suddenly grabbed it and put it into his own pocket.

"Here are the shoes," he said, taking down a curious pair of shoes from a shelf behind the door. They were bright yellow, and had turned-up ends of red painted iron to kick with. The two brownies took them eagerly. They thanked the gnome and turned to go.

"Bring them back to-night without fail," commanded Grumpy. He shook his head fiercely at them. Making all the silver bells tinkle again, and then slammed the door.

"What an unpleasant creature he is, to be sure," said Skip, looking quite pale. "I was really afraid he was going to turn us into black-beetles or something! You

know, he is supposed to do that to people he doesn't like. And once he turned a cheeky pixie into a currant bun and ate him! Ooooh my, he's a horrid person!"

The brownies hurried home with the magic shoes. When they got there they each put a shoe on their right foot and danced about in glee.

"We've got the Kickaway Shoes, we've got the Kickaway Shoes!" they cried. They made such a noise that Whiskers, their big black cat, came out to see what they were doing.

He stood behind the saucepan, lifted his right foot and gave the saucepan an enormous kick with the iron end of the Kickaway Shoe! Bang!

The saucepan shot into the air and flew away! My, how it flew! The brownies watched it going through the air until it was just a black speck. Then they couldn't see it any longer.

"I wonder where it's gone to?" said Jump.

"It's gone to the Land of Rubbish," said Skip. "Now it's your turn, Jump. Kick that vase away!"

Jump kicked with all his might. The vase broke into a hundred pieces, and each piece flew through the air at top speed.

They soon disappeared. The brownies giggled. This was great fun!

"We'll both kick away this nasty old bedstead," said Skip. "It's so big it wants two people to kick it, I'm sure!"

"Hello, Whiskers, darling!" cried the brownies, who were both very fond of their cat. "Look at our magic shoes."

Whiskers sniffed them and hurriedly backed away. She had smelt the magic in them and was afraid. She went off to a corner of the garden.

"Now let's start kicking away all our rubbish!" cried Skip. "Come on! Watch me kick away this old saucepan!"

They both kicked with all their might. At once the bedstead rose into the air, and to the great delight of the brownies, and to the enormous surprise of the pixies down in the village, the old iron bedstead flew through the air, looking smaller and

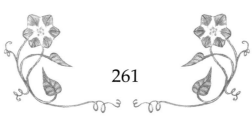

smaller the further it
flew. It was
most exciting.

The brownies laughed
till the tears came into
their eyes. They were
having a glorious time.
They kicked away the
candlesticks, the old
boots and the tin kettles.
They kicked away a pile
of books and a broken
spade. They kicked dozens of things and
shouted in glee when they saw them all
flying off in the air, never to come back.

At last there was nothing but an old
basket left. Skip gave it a hard kick, and it
rose into the air – but oh, goodness, what
a dreadful thing! Whiskers, the cat, had
curled herself up in that basket and Skip
didn't know that she was there! When the
basket rose up in the air Whiskers shot
out and she and the basket flew along
together at top speed!

Whiskers mewed loudly, but it was no
use. She had to go to the Land of
Rubbish, and soon the horrified brownies
could see nothing of her but a tiny speck
far away in the sky.

"Oh! Oh!" cried Skip, the tears running
down his cheeks in two streams. "I didn't
know Whiskers was in the basket! She'll
never come back! Oh, my dear, darling
old cat! Oh, Jump, she's gone!"

Jump sobbed, too. Both brownies loved their cat with all their hearts, and it was dreadful to think poor old Whiskers had been kicked off to the Land of Rubbish. How upset she would be! How lonely and frightened!

"Who will g-g-g-give her her m-m-m-m-milk?" wept Skip.

"Who will t-t-t-t-tuck her up in a warm rug at night?" sobbed Jump.

It was dreadful. The brownies couldn't think what to do! They put their arms round one another and cried so much that they made a puddle around their feet.

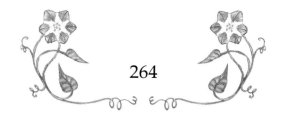

At last Skip had an idea.

"Let's go to Grumpy Gnome and ask him to tell us how to get Whiskers back!" he said. "There is sure to be a spell to get her back."

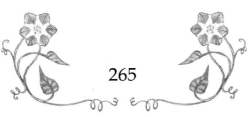

"Yes, yes!" cried Jump, wiping his eyes with his big yellow handkerchief. So off they set once more to Grumpy's cottage.

The gnome frowned at them when he opened the door. "I said bring back the shoes to-night, not this afternoon," he said crossly. "I was just having a nap and you've wakened me."

"Oh, please, Grumpy, we've come about something terribly important," said Skip. "We've kicked Whiskers, our lovely black cat, away by mistake, and we want you to tell us how to get her back!"

Grumpy's little eyes gleamed. "Ha!" he thought. "I can make some money out of this."

"Well," he said aloud, "that's certainly very serious. You will have to pay me a very large sum of money to get her back. It's very hard to get a black cat back from the Land of Rubbish."

"Oh dear," said Jump and Skip. "How much money do you want?"

"I want fifty pieces of gold!" said Grumpy."

"Ooooooo!" squealed Skip and Jump in horror. "We only have three pieces! Get us our cat back for three pieces, Grumpy."

"Certainly not," said the gnome, pretending that he was shutting the door. "Fifty pieces, or no cat!"

"Wait, wait!" said Jump. "We've only three pieces, I tell you. What else will you take besides our three pieces of gold?"

"Well, I'll take your grandfather clock," said Grumpy.

"Oh!" groaned the brownies sorrowfully. "We do so love our old clock. But you shall have it."

"And your rocking-chair," said Grumpy. "And the pair of lovely brass candlesticks you have on your mantlepiece."

The brownies groaned again. They were proud of their rocking-chair and candlesticks. But still, they loved Whiskers more than all these things, so they sadly promised to go back home and fetch the gold, the clock, the chair and the candlesticks at once.

They ran off, crying. What a dreadful thing to have to give up all their nicest things to the horrid, greedy gnome! If he had been at all kind-hearted he would have been sorry about Whiskers, and would have got her back for nothing. But, oh, the Grumpy Gnome had a heart as hard as stone!

Skip and Jump fetched out their big clock, their old rocking-chair, and the two candlesticks. Skip had the gold in his pocket. He carried the rocking-chair, too. Jump managed to take the grandfather clock and the candlesticks. They went slowly along, panting and puffing under their heavy loads.

Just as they got near Grumpy's cottage they met Bron, the head brownie of the village. He was most astonished to see Skip and jump carrying such heavy things.

"Are you moving?" he asked.

"No," said Skip. "We are taking these things to Grumpy." Then he told Bron all that had happened, and how Grumpy had made them promise to give him their nicest things in return for getting back Whiskers from the Land of Rubbish.

"So that's why we are taking him out three gold pieces, our beautiful grandfather clock, our rocking-chair and our lovely candlesticks," said Skip sadly. "But you see, we must get Whiskers back. She'll be lonely and so frightened."

Bron frowned and looked as black as thunder when he heard about the greed and selfishness of the unkind gnome.

"Where are the Kickaway Shoes?" he asked.

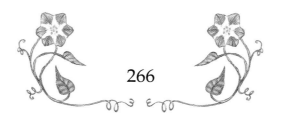

"I've still got one on, and so has Skip," said Jump, and he lifted up his right foot to show Bron.

"Give them to me," said Bron.

In great surprise Skip and Jump took of the Kickaway Shoes and watched Bron put them on, one on each foot.

Then they looked on in greater surprise when he marched straight up to Grumpy's front door and banged hard on the knocker.

"RAT-A-TAT-TAT!"

The door flew open and out came Grumpy, looking very angry indeed.

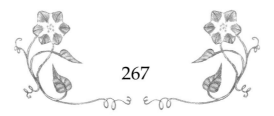

"How dare you knock so loudly!" he began, in a rage – then he stopped when he saw it was Bron knocking and not Skip and Jump.

"I've just come to tell you something, Grumpy Gnome," said Bron, in a very fierce voice. "I've come to tell you that you are the nastiest, greediest, unkindest gnome in the whole of the kingdom, and you don't deserve to live in this nice little village."

"Oh, don't I?" said Grumpy, his little eyes glittering wickedly. "Well, where do I deserve to live then? Tell me that!" And he turned to go indoors again.

"The best place for you is the Land of Rubbish!" shouted Bron and, before

"Don't worry!" said Bron cheerfully. "A cat can always find its way home again, no matter where it's taken to. Whiskers will come back all right – and that wicked gnome knew it perfectly well. He was just robbing you of all these things for nothing. Take them back home again, put down a saucer of milk, and wait for Whiskers to come back."

"Oh, thank you, Bron," said the grateful little brownies. "But what are you going to do with the Kickaway Shoes?"

"I shall keep them in my house, and then if anyone wants to borrow them he can do so for nothing," said Bron. He put on his own shoes, and then, taking the Kickaway Shoes under his arm, he went off home, whistling loudly. He stopped every now and then to laugh when he thought of the Grumpy Gnome sailing through the air to the Land of Rubbish!

Grumpy could get inside the door, he kicked him hard with the iron points of the Kickaway Shoes – first with one shoe and then with the other.

Oh, my goodness me! Grumpy gave a loud yell and rose up into the air, and then, still yelling, he flew on and on to the Land of Rubbish. The brownies watched him – and then suddenly Skip gave a cry.

"Oh, Bron! You've kicked him away before he told us how to get back dear old Whiskers. Oh dear, oh dear!"

Skip and Jump staggered home again with all their belongings. They put them back in their places, and then they went to the larder for some milk. They poured out a saucerful,

269

and put it down on the floor, ready for Whiskers when she came back.

Then they put the kettle on for tea, and toasted some muffins, for they really felt very hungry.

And would you believe it, just as they were sitting down to eat their tea, there came a mewing at the door! Skip leapt up and opened it – and there outside was dear old Whiskers, very tired and very hungry, for she had walked a very long way indeed.

"Darling old Whiskers!" cried the brownies in delight, hugging her and stroking her soft fur. "Oh, we are glad to see you! Here's some milk for you! And shall we open a tin of sardines for you, just for a treat?"

They were all so happy that evening. Whiskers sat on Skip's knee first, and then on Jump's, so that they might share her properly between them. She was just as glad to be back home again as they were to have her.

As for Grumpy Gnome, he's still in the Land of Rubbish. And a very good place for him, too!

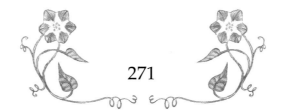

Nippy the Pixie

Nippy the pixie was a tiresome fellow. He had long strong fingers, and he loved to nip and pinch people with them. He had long toes, and he liked to kick slyly under the table. He liked to poke people too, and to tread on their toes. He was not a very pleasant fellow.

One day he was very pleased. He had an invitation to a party! It was to be a seaside party, and Nippy thought that would be most exciting. Scaly the merman had asked him to the party. Nippy felt sure he would have a fine time.

He dressed himself in his best, got on his bicycle, and rode off. It wasn't very far to the sea. He would be at the party just in time!

Scaly was there to greet him. He shook hands politely, and asked Nippy into his rock-pool, which was most beautifully decorated with seaweed and anemones.

Nippy dipped his hands into the water, rubbed them over his face, and muttered a few magic words. He could now go under the water without being wet! He could breathe there, too. It was a marvellous spell.

Nippy followed Scaly into the pool. The seaweed fluttered round. The shells made a pretty floor, laid in a neat pattern over the sand. There was a table made of rock, and on it were all sorts of exciting things to eat!

"Where are the other guests?" asked Nippy, looking round.

"They will be here in a minute," said Scaly; and, sure enough, they all swam up or crawled up as he finished speaking.

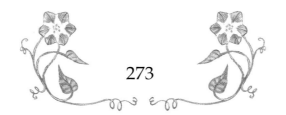

They were strange guests. There was a large yellow crab, and there were three small green crabs. There was a great lobster, a rather alarming fellow. There were six shrimps and six prawns, all neat and shining. There was a fat jellyfish with ribbons hanging down from his umbrella-like body. Nippy didn't much like the look of them.

They all knew Nippy. They shook hands with him, and nodded. "Ah, Nippy!" they said. "We have heard of you! Yes – we have heard of you!"

Nippy felt rather pleased. He hadn't known he was so famous!

"Pray, sit down!" said Scaly, the merman, beckoning his guests to the rock-table, on which there were sea-cakes, seaweed lemonade, sea-spray ice-cream with foam on the top, and rock-biscuits, hard outside and sweet inside.

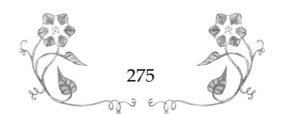

Everyone sat down. Nippy sat next to one of the little green crabs. Opposite him was the lobster. Nippy looked hungrily at the cakes. He pinched the little crab next to him in excitement. "Isn't this fun!" he said.

The crab opened a pair of his pincers and pinched Nippy back. "Ooooh!" said Nippy, startled. "Don't do that. It hurts!"

"But you did it to me," said the crab smiling, and looking at Nippy with his stalked eyes. "It's a fine game, this nipping and pinching. That's why Scaly asked you to his party – you are the only pixie he knows who can nip and pinch and poke as we can. He thought you would enjoy it very much."

"Oh," said Nippy, feeling rather alarmed.

The big lobster opposite beamed at him and put a pair of his enormous claws under the table. He felt about for Nippy's bare knee and nipped it hard.

"Ooooh!" said Nippy. "Don't!"

"You can nip me back," said the lobster. "Go on, Nippy; pinch me hard. We love it, you know."

"*We* like poking people with the sharp needles in our heads," said a large prawn suddenly to the pixie. "Like this, Nippy!"

The prawn dug the surprised pixie in the chest with his sharp needle, and Nippy gave a yell and fell off his chair. Another shrimp poked him hard.

Then the big yellow crab pinched each of his toes in turn. What fun those creatures had!

"I don't like it, I don't like it!" wept Nippy. "Please stop them, Scaly."

"But this is their idea of fun," said the merman. "I thought it was yours, too, Nippy. I have often heard how you pinch, nip, kick, and poke people, so I thought you'd love my party. Please don't spoil it. Go and nip everyone else. Crabs and lobsters love that kind of game."

"But they are so hard to nip!" wept Nippy. "And they can nip me much harder than I can nip them. It isn't fair."

277

Just at that moment the jellyfish left its place and floated over to Nippy. "Play with me, pixie," it said, in a soft, shivery voice. It let down its ribbon-streamers all round the pixie, and Nippy gave a yell.

"You're stinging me, you're stinging me!" he cried. "Go away!"

"Come on, boys, let's have a fine game with this silly pixie!" cried the big lobster. And, to Nippy's horror, all the shrimps, prawns, crabs, lobster, and jellyfish surrounded him and began to have a horrid sort of game with him.

They pinched him and nipped him and pricked him and poked him and stung him till Nippy rushed out of the pool, jumped on his bicycle, and rode back home, crying bitterly.

"It was a horrid, horrid party!" he wept. "Scaly was silly to think I'd like a pinching party with all those sea-creatures!"

He sat down at home and made himself a cup of cocoa and took some biscuits from a tin, for he had had no tea at all. He thought hard as he nibbled and drank.

"I hated that pinching and poking," he thought. "How other people must have hated *my* pinching and poking too! I'll never do it again, never!"

He didn't tell anyone about Scaly's pinching party, but they all knew – because Scaly told them! How they laughed and laughed!

"Nippy won't try his old tricks again!" they said. And he didn't He keeps his fingers to himself now – and a good thing, too! If you know anyone who is a pincher or poker, just let Scaly know – he'll arrange a nice little party for them, you may be sure!

The Real Live Fairy Doll

Gwen and Peter were very much excited because they were going to have a big Christmas tree that Christmas. What fun!

"Will it have a fairy doll at the top, Mummy?" asked Gwen. "I do hope it will."

"You shall have a fairy doll at the very top!" said Mummy, "and lots of toys and candles all over the tree."

That night Daddy and Mummy went out to buy the tree and all the things to hang on it. They bought the prettiest fairy doll you ever saw, with wings of silver, and a dress that shone and glittered. She was to go at the top of the tree.

All the toys were hung on the tree, and the candles were slipped into their stands and clipped to the branches. The doll was fastened to the very tip, and how grand she looked, shining there. Mummy and Daddy were very pleased.

The toys in the nursery sat and looked at the tree in delight, when Mummy and Daddy had gone downstairs. They thought they had never in all their life seen such a pretty thing. As for the fairy doll, they thought she was the loveliest toy in the world.

Then a most dreadful thing happened. What do you think? The poor fairy doll was not fastened tightly enough to the tree, and suddenly she felt herself falling!

"Help! Help!" she squealed.

But nobody could help her. She fell – she slid between the branches of the Christmas tree and landed with a bump on the floor.

All the toys rushed to pick her up.

But oh, dear me, she had broken both her nice little legs! What a dreadful thing!

"Whatever shall we do?" said the teddy bear. "Is there time for her to be mended before the children have the tree tomorrow night?"

"Let's go and ask the elf who lives under the nursery window," said the toy soldier. "She knows a lot. Perhaps she could mend the fairy doll."

So they called her in. She came dancing into the nursery and looked at the poor broken doll crying on the floor.

"I will take her to the Mend-Up Gnome," she said. "He will soon mend her nicely. She will be quite all right in twenty-four hours' time."

"Twenty-four hours!" cried the toys. "Goodness, won't the children be disappointed. They *did* so want a fairy doll to stand at the top of their Christmas tree tomorrow night!"

Everyone stood looking very gloomy – and then the toy soldier spoke up. He turned to the elf and said: "I say! Would *you* take the fairy doll's place do you think? You have silvery wings like hers and your dress is all shiny and glittering too. You would have a fine time at the top of the tree and you would see everything that was going on."

"Well," said the elf, thoughtfully, "well – let me see. Yes – I think I could do that for you. I love boys and girls and it would be fun to see them all dancing round the tree and having their presents. I'll just take this doll to old Mend-Up, and then I'll come back and fly up to the top of the tree!"

You should have seen how lovely she looked up there! The toys looked and looked at her – and when the party began the next day, how all the children stared to see such a beautiful fairy doll at the top of the tree!

"It's a real, live fairy; that's what it is," said another little girl. "It's not a doll at all!"

She had a lovely time. She watched the children dancing – and do you know what she did when the grown-ups had gone out of the room to have some supper, and had left the children by themselves? She flew down from the tree, took hands with them and danced all round the tree, singing a little magic song in a high, silvery voice.

The children were surprised and pleased.

"I say! That's a wonderful fairy doll of yours!" said one little girl to Gwen. "My doll talks and walks, but I've never seen one that could dance and sing!"

Just then the elf heard the grown-ups coming and she flew straight back to the top of the tree.

"Mummy!" cried Gwen. "Do you know, the fairy doll flew down from the tree and danced and sang with us!"

"Nonsense!" said Mummy, and nobody would believe that what the children said was true.

"Well," said Gwen to Peter, "when Mummy takes the fairy doll down from the tree to-morrow, she will find it is a real live fairy – and won't she be surprised?"

But the little fairy doll came back from Mend-Up the Gnome's that night, both her legs beautifully mended, and the toys helped her to climb to the top of the tree. The elf flew down and said good-bye to the toys.

"I *have* enjoyed myself!" she said. "And wasn't it fun when I flew down and danced with the children? I nearly laughed out loud to see their surprised faces!"

The next day the children begged their mother to take down the fairy doll from the tree. They felt quite sure it was a *real* fairy, and not a doll. But when they saw her, what a disappointment!

"It's a doll after all!" said Gwen. "I wonder how it was she turned into a live fairy last night."

"Don't be silly," said Mummy, laughing. "I don't know why you keep telling that foolish story, Gwen. No fairy doll could come down from the tree and dance and sing."

"Well, it *must* have been a fairy then," said Peter. "So that settles it!"

He was quite right, wasn't he?

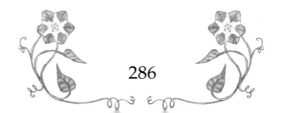